Concrete Alibi

- a murder mystery set in Glasgow

M. MacGregor

Published in 2017 by
Moira Brown
Broughty Ferry
Dundee. DD5 2HZ
www.publishkindlebooks4u.co.uk

Concrete Alibi was first published
as a kindle book in 2016.

ISBN13: 978 1 52078 014 6

About the author

The author was brought up in Fife, Scotland and at various times has dabbled in comedy writing. Programme makers at BBC Radio Scotland have offered encouragement.

Acknowledgements

A special thanks to my informal, enthusiastic team of editors/supporters who gave me valuable feedback after reading that rusty first draft. They are Jim & Ann Buist, Jim Hewiston, Dorothy Spencer, my supportive husband Eric and Columbo-loving brother-in-law Christopher.

Disclaimer

This is a work of fiction. Names, characters, businesses, places, events and incidents are either a product of the author's imagination or being used in a fictitious manner.

PART ONE
BUILDING UP TO MURDER

Mackintosh Lecture

'It was Charles Rennie Mackintosh's unique way of blending decorative interiors with stark, practical exteriors that helped create his highly individual architectural style.'

As he delivers his lecture the professor tosses back his floppy grey hair and smiles an all-knowing smile. Professor Baird is confident he looks good tonight in his black slacks, polo-neck sweater and trademark Le Corbusier, thick-rimmed glasses. He has a lot in common with the deceased Swiss architect, especially his high opinion of himself.

'So I hope I've been able to shed some light on why Charles Rennie Mackintosh is today considered one of the best Scottish architects who ever lived. Now, if there are no more questions I'll end it there.'

A middle-aged man, possibly a journalist, raises his hand. 'Is it true you've been nominated for the *Mackintosh Life Time Achievement Award*?'

The audience turns in the direction of the deep, attractive Glaswegian voice, much richer than the professor's, and one that would not be out of place in a professional theatre. Feigning embarrassment the professor responds,

'Yes, I have.' He smooths his hair in case anyone considers taking a photograph. No one does.

'Do you know when they are likely to announce the winner?'

'Yes, in two days' time at the awards ceremony in the Blythswood Square Hotel.'

Professor Baird parts his confident lips and makes a lousy attempt at modesty. 'There are other equally talented architects up for the award. Let's wait and see shall we? Unless, that is, you have a crystal ball?'

The audience laughs and the jovial atmosphere is set for the drinks reception. Professor Baird retreats from the spotlight and grabs a glass of wine from the side-lines offered to him on a silver tray by a former student who has had to retrain as a wine waiter due to a slump in construction. He has volunteered to work for free tonight in the hope of making contacts in the business. Within minutes the professor is surrounded by admirers.

'What a wonderful lecture, Professor Baird,' the young, elegant Asian woman enthuses. 'I'm thinking what a travesty it is that I've lived in Glasgow all my life and have never visited Hill House in Helensburgh. It looks amazing and you say Brad Pitt has been there twice?'

'Yes, I believe he fell in love with it as we all do.'

Somehow, despite a predominantly older gathering, the professor always manages to mingle with the younger, more impressionable, sycophantic set. Yet despite enjoying the attention, his eyes dart about the room as if looking for someone. They relax when he catches sight of the waiter walking towards them. Professor Baird seizes the opportunity to swap his empty glass with a full one.

Detective Inspector Lorna Gunn, a stylish woman interested in the arts, is one of the more discerning members of the audience. She has decided, based on the professor's lecture, this particular society is not for her. Arriving at this conclusion, she sees no point in making an effort to socialise with people she's unlikely to ever meet again.

The Blythswood

'This is a most striking building. I have wonderful memories of coming here as a boy.' The professor is standing in the impressive foyer of the Blythswood Square hotel surrounded by students chosen by him to attend the awards ceremony.

Looking upwards, the flock of students gape wide-eyed at the beautiful classical architecture surrounding them.

'Has it changed much since you were a lad?' asks a cheery first year student from Yorkshire.

'Oh aye, it was the RAC club then – an exclusive private members' club. They didn't let in any riff raff...' He grins, '... and that meant no women.'

'What does RAC stand for?' asks a female student, with the good sense to change the subject, gazing admiringly at him.

'It stands for the Royal Automobile Club and that's why the images inside the lampshades and other interior decorations throughout the hotel have an automobile theme. In the olden days Blythswood Square was one of the starting points of the Monte Carlo Car Rally. Thousands of people lined the streets for the send-off.'

'That is so cool,' responds an attractive nineteen-year-old, wearing a strapless dress showing off her ample cleavage. Emily is one of the professor's favourites.

A tall, slim woman, draped in a waist-length fox fur coat, is ushered out of the cold and into the warm, grand entrance hall by the friendly, outlandishly-dressed doorman. This is a hotel where those with high disposable incomes are made most welcome.

The woman strides across the hall, her designer heels clicking against the hard marble-tiled floor as she goes. Pausing at the top of a short flight of stairs leading down to the main bar, her eyes scan the enormous, sumptuous room looking for her husband.

'Richard!'

The professor, by now with a large gin and tonic in his hand, is lapping up the mellow atmosphere the Bossa Nova Jazz has helped create. He turns around to see his wife walking towards him.

'You took your time.'

'I couldn't get parked anywhere.'

Trudy takes a mineral water offered to her by a smart, uniformed barman who happens to be the same young man who was on serving duties, just days earlier, at the Mackintosh lecture. Richard pays little attention to minions so has failed to notice.

'That's the last time I bring the car into the city centre.'

Trudy had reluctantly agreed to drive tonight after having disgraced herself at a previous award's ceremony. Under the influence of alcohol she can occasionally let slip her working-class roots, unlike her husband, who, brought up three streets away in Dennistoun, performs as if he were reared in the land of gentry. Yet, he never lies. The professor had visited the RAC gentleman's club as a boy. He was signed in by his childhood friend Edmund whose father was a successful Glasgow solicitor.

It was thanks to Edmund's father that Richard had secured a job in an architect's office on leaving school. He had qualified as an architect by attending art college on a part-time basis.

The close friendship between the boys ended when Richard, aged twenty, stole Edmund's girlfriend Trudy. Indeed Trudy stands by her husband's side tonight demonstrating her loyalty and commitment, unwavering after thirty-eight years of marriage.

Finally, the architects and their wives and a few solitary husbands attached to female architects, make their way through to the banqueting hall.

*

'Drum roll please? And the winner is...' The President of the Institute of Scottish Architects pauses for dramatic effect as the audience waits with bated breath. He smiles cheekily as he looks around the room. All eyes are focused on him.

'I'm afraid you'll have to wait a moment longer...' A big sigh reverberates around the room as the audience unlocks its gaze '... because we have invited Margo Mackintosh, a direct descendent of Charles Rennie, to present this prestigious award.'

A mousy, middle-aged woman, lacking the grace, style and looks of her famous ancestor, rushes in carrying a glass, art deco trophy and positions herself behind the microphone.

'The winner of the Mackintosh Lifetime Achievement Award is ... Professor Richard Baird.'

The room erupts into applause.

'Where is Professor Baird?' A spotlight searches the room and lands on the great man. The professor is already on his feet, winning speech in hand, embracing his wife.

The crowd chant predictably, 'SPEECH! SPEECH!' as the professor takes the triumphant walk to the front where the microphone and stand are positioned. He flicks back his silvery hair as he goes, aware he will almost certainly be photographed tonight. The press must surely be present.

The great-niece of Charles Rennie Mackintosh, mutters, 'Professor Baird, congratulations!' as she places the glass trophy into his outstretched, soft, chubby hands which have never known a hard day's work.

'Thank you, my dear. It will find a special place in my collection.'

Architecture has been good to Professor Baird. Having benefited from the post-war building boom and enjoyed a modicum of recognition for his bold, modernist designs he had secured the top job when the new architecture school was established in Glasgow. The charmed, secure, prestigious job with gold-plated pension carrying the "professor" title turned out to be so cushy he was even able to continue practicing.

Professor Baird's earnings in a bad recession like the current one, were causing a great deal of resentment amongst jobbing architects or "cad monkeys" as the younger architects tended to call themselves.

The crowd gradually ceases clapping and makes itself comfortable in preparation for, what they suspect, may be a long speech.

'Ladies, gentlemen, I am truly honoured (and humbled) to be the first ever recipient of this award. But firstly, I'd like to thank…'

Professor Baird drones on so long that people begin to fidget and whisper. The younger set play with their smart phones underneath the table. One elderly gentleman falls asleep.

'Well, that's all I wanted to say, except to thank my wonderful wife who has supported me every step of the way.'

Professor Baird hands back the microphone and, responding to the cue, the audience clap loudly. The attendees, mostly just there to party, are relieved when he finally sits down.

The President concludes, 'In case anyone is unaware, the Clydeview Holiday Resort, one of Professor Baird's architectural gems, will be open to the public this coming Saturday as part of the

Open Doors Festival. And at one o'clock, weather permitting, Professor Baird will give a short talk from the cinema foyer area. I say "weather permitting" as most of you will be aware the building is now somewhat derelict and no longer has a roof.' A few participants snigger. 'There's little room for cars up at the resort so the architecture school is kindly providing a double-decker bus. It will depart from the school's main entrance at noon on Saturday.'

The formalities complete, chattering returns at the large round tables as the attendees are, at last given an opportunity to discuss their thoughts on whether or not Richard Baird is a worthy winner.

The young wine waiter rushes around the room topping up the glasses of those who clearly have a taste for the drink, disappearing temporarily only to return with another bottle.

'I knew they'd give it to that big-head. As if he hasn't had enough praise already in his life,' complains a young architect beginning to slur her words.

'Oh, come on, hun. We were just born in the wrong era... and we were definitely born the wrong sex.'

'Someone needs to get rid of the misogynistic git.' The female architect points a thin index finger in the direction of Professor Baird, then she motions to the wine waiter she'd like a top-up. 'My uncle told me not to become an architect. He warned me it's all peaks and troughs.'

'Yeh, there's plenty of troughs, not so may peaks though.'

'But would I listen?'

Watching as the liquid pours into her glass, her friend replies, mournfully,

'Young people never listen.'

At another table, some middle-aged male architects gossip excitedly about dodgy judging decisions Professor Baird has been involved in. Recently he announced Edwin Jones, his favourite past pupil, as the competition winner selected to design the Scottish government's luxury spa extension.

'My firm's design was easily the best and he chose that horrific concrete block that looks like a public toilet you'd be frightened to piss in. He's like the Scottish Mafia of the built environment.'

'Yer preaching to the converted, Ciaran. We know.'

'He always favours architects who went to his school; people who copy his horrid, brutalist style. It's an absolute disgrace.' Ciaran takes another glug of brandy.

'Ciaran, we know.'

'Look how Charles Rennie Mackintosh was treated in his home city and they have the nerve to name the award after him.'

'Change the record, Ciaran.'

'Have you seen his grave in Golders Green crematorium in London?'

'No, but I've got a feeling you have.'

'The only sign marking his grave is a small, cheap plastic plaque stuck in the earth. The poor guy died in poverty.'

'Come on Ciaran, let's order a taxi.'

'We're not going to see a change in Scotland until that man is six feet under. I tell ye, I'll be celebrating the day he snuffs it.'

Elsewhere in the Monte Carlo suite similar heated debates take place out of earshot of Professor Baird who sits admiring at his trophy.

*

'This is ridiculous. Whose great idea was this anyway?' Trudy Baird asks as she struggles along the uneven, overgrown path leading to the collection of crumbling, austere buildings which once provided a peaceful haven for young families on holiday.

'I suppose it was yours.' Trudy throws an accusatory glance at her husband.

'I can't help it if people are fascinated by my work.' Richard impatiently strides ahead. He battles on through the nettles and wild flowers towards their destination.

Trudy gasps and grabs her husband's arm.

'What is it now?'

'It's horrific.'

'What is?' Professor Baird follows his wife's gaze to witness a spectacular but hideous sight; vegetation sprouts through a concrete shell covered in fluorescent multi-coloured graffiti. They have finally arrived at the professor's architectural masterpiece.

Sophie complains, 'I can't believe I'm giving up my Saturday to come here and I wouldn't be surprised if the buildings are riddled with asbestos.'

'Look, they wouldn't have brought us here if they didn't think it was safe,' replies Angus.

'They get us to do all sorts of things that aren't safe.'

'Such as?'

'Making models using scalpel knives. They're lethal.'

'Sophie, you know why we had to come. The guy in fifth year wasn't joking when he said if we want to pass the course we'd better keep in with Professor Baird. He said, "Forget reading books just suck up to the professor".'

'Oh... Oh my God!' Sophie's eyes become enlarged and almost burst out of her creative head.

There, in front of them, not one hundred yards away, are the brutalist, concrete buildings they have heard Professor Baird boast so much about during their first semester at architecture school. But in real life the abandoned collection of buildings are much much much creepier and uglier than in the YouTube videos.

'Sophie. How many signatures did you say were on the petition to save this place?'

'Thirty-four.'

'I don't know about you but I'm wishing I hadn't signed it.'

Bernard Hughes, the Health and Safety Officer in charge, ensures that all those present are led safely into the foyer area of the cinema building. An empty lectern faces rows of seating gradually filling up with people keen to hear what the eminent architect has to say. Visitors either love or hate Clydeview Holiday Resort but it's difficult to judge in its current state whether or not it should be demolished. If it were "done up" it would certainly look a lot better.

Professor Baird, on the stroke of one o'clock, on hearing a signal gong, approaches the lectern. A ray of sunlight filters directly onto him through a round light well above, now devoid of a piece of glazing.

'I hope you'll forgive me today if at any point I burst into tears.' Professor Baird casts his eyes around him taking in the horror of the interior. 'Visiting here today reminds me of our recent study trip to Detroit. It is a reminder to us all that buildings are nothing without the will of the people to use and maintain them.'

The professor's disciples smile and nod in agreement. He continues in a subdued fashion,

'To give you a chance to roam about yourselves, I'm going to keep this fairly brief... '

A man jumps to his feet, pointing upwards, 'Watch out!!!'

Richard Baird looks up, 'What's the mat...'

A huge block of concrete crashes down on him taking his body to the ground with it. A spontaneous choir erupts as each member instinctively finds his or her own unique, terrifying sound signaling disaster. Hands cover faces. Heads turn away. A young student faints. Trudy collapses. The deafening sound of the screaming ensemble causes wildlife to flee from the recesses of the eerie building. The ugly noise conveniently drowns out the unpleasant sound of the professor gurgling blood, his body shaking and convulsing. Finally the motion in his body stops.

The brave Health and Safety Officer bolts forward to survey the carnage. He stares down at the professor's face strewn with blood and his mashed up, lifeless body. None of his first aid training has prepared him for this.

A woman pushes past him muttering,

'Get out of my way. I'm a nurse.'

Moving over to the unsightly body, she bends down and taking hold of his wrist feels for a pulse. There is none. The professor's wife cries hysterically into a man's chest. The nurse catches the man's eyes. She shakes her head and says in a barely audible voice, 'He's dead'.

PART TWO
THE INVESTIGATION

The first police officers to appear at the scene are Constables Adams and Steele. They congratulate the Health and Safety Officer for cordoning off the area and reinforce this with blue and white tape before clambering up to the floor above to mark out the area around the skylight.

Within an hour of the incident the Clydeview Resort resembles a somber crime scene. Helping to create this morbid image are Scenes of Crime Officers (or SOCOs) who, fully kitted out in polythene costume, carefully photograph and gather evidence.

Adams and Steele are finishing taking statements when Detective Inspector Lorna Gunn and her sidekick, Detective Constable Alistair Boyle, appear on the scene. Alistair, fit as a fiddle, hasn't broken sweat during his trek up the hill; however, middle-aged DI Gunn is hunched over holding a hand on each knee desperately trying to regain her breath while taking in the horror of what lies before them. She notices a pair of thick, round, black-framed glasses lying mangled amongst the debris. Her eyes are drawn to the equally mangled body. The face is unrecognisable, the hair matted with blood, but the clothes seem vaguely familiar. DI Gunn twigs that the dead architect lying out ungainly in front of her, is the same man she almost died of boredom listening to only five days earlier.

They make their way to speak to their uniformed colleagues.

'I'm DI Lorna Gunn and this is DC Boyle.'

Steele's voice conveys relief. 'Boy, are we glad to see you.'

'What are you first thoughts? Do you think it was an accident?'

'Could have been but it's not likely.'

'What makes you think that?'

Adams elaborates, 'Well, a block of concrete fell through the hole in the ceiling directly above the body.'

'And?'

'And... the ceiling hasn't collapsed so someone or something must have pushed it over the edge.'

Steele interjects, 'We cannae be certain but it looks like... the guy wiz murdered.'

'We've cordoned off the whole area above too. We took the wife's statement first and arranged for a police car to take her home.'

'Good. Now I need to change into a SOCO suit and take a look myself.' She turns to Alistair, 'If you could speak with some of the witnesses.'

'The bus is about to leave, boss. Should I travel back to Glasgow with them?'

'Yes. You do that.'

'How are yez doing?' Alistair flashes his police badge and sits sideways in a seat in front of two female students.

'How d'you think we're doing?' replies Paula as she scrapes back her curly brown hair before securing it again in a ponytail high up at the back of her head. 'We've just seen a horrible accident.'

'Must have been pretty nasty to witness,' replies Alistair.

'Positively ghastly.'

'I hear he was quite a famous architect.'

'Ya. He was mega talented. Last week he won the *Mackintosh Lifetime Achievement Award*.'

'Really? And was he head guy at your school?'

'Ya, he was due to mark our final year crits.'

The other girl cries half-heartedly. 'Now I'll never know if he liked my visitor centre in Inverkip.'

'Okay, girls. Thanks for your help.'

Alistair moves to the top deck and listens in to several conversations bemoaning the loss while others have already moved on. Two men debate whether they'll be home in time to catch the t.v. quiz programme *Pointless*.

'That's me away now,' the police doctor says cheerily after confirming death and arranging for the body to be moved to the mortuary. He is keen to rejoin his family at the five star Cameron House Hotel situated on the banks of Loch Lomond. He imagines relaxing in the sauna and cleansing himself of all this blood and gore.

DI Gunn isn't so lucky. She braces herself for a long night ahead as she knows the first seventy-two hours after a crime has been committed are the most crucial in solving it.

DI Gunn stands in the incident room drinking a large latte from a paper cup. Several police officers sit before her awaiting instruction, painfully aware this could turn into a long, tiring case because they don't, as yet, have a single suspect.

Lorna has already met with her own boss, Detective Chief Inspector Darren Russell, who has confirmed what little manpower he is prepared to set aside for the case. And with the recent cut backs and threat of outsourcing forensics she didn't need to be reminded how important it is she solves this case as soon as possible.

DI Gunn has to put up with this type of repetitive chat on a daily basis and is sick of propping him up, including rewriting statements before he releases them to the press. She can't wait for Darren Russell to retire in two years' time and wishes the Thornliebank Masonic Lodge had, in the past, been a bit more selective with their intake.

'Now, until we receive evidence back from forensics to suggest otherwise we are treating this as a murder enquiry.' Lorna takes a sip of the huge, calorie-laden latte which likely explains why her clothes' size has gradually increased over the years rather than her own flamboyant explanation which is to blame her Taurean star sign. Yet, despite her less than taut stomach, DI Gunn still has a strong, shapely body topped with a lively good-looking face – a face still adored by her husband Colin, a strong, gentle man and part-time librarian who had to resign from the drug squad because arresting poor people was adversely affecting his health.

Sergeant Jenny Brown, a bright spark with a degree in Law, reminds DI Gunn, 'But there have been accidents before at the resort, boss.'

'Yes, I know, Jenny, but it seems highly improbable the concrete block dislodged itself. The block weighed 27 kg. The ceiling didn't collapse so someone strong must have pushed it.'

Lorna picks up a photographic print and pins it to a board. 'And this photograph shows a fresh footprint found right next to the hole in the floor above. By close of Monday forensics will be able to tell us the size of the footprint, the type of shoe or boot and roughly the weight of the person wearing them. Ah, here comes Alistair.'

DC Boyle enters the room carrying golf clubs.

'He has his priorities right.' The others laugh.

Alistair sniggers as he lays the clubs down and takes a seat, 'I'd already booked a lesson at lunch-time.'

'Did you manage to find out anything interesting about our victim, Professor Baird?'

'Not really, boss. Only that he had received the *Mackintosh Life Time Achievement Award* only days before at a posh bash at The Blythswood.'

'What's that?'

'It's some top architecture award given to him by RISA?'

'Plain Scottish please, Alistair.'

'The Royal Institute of Scottish Architects.'

'Oh, a Royal Institute. Swanky.'

'Aye. And everyone I spoke to on the bus seemed to think the sun shone out of the professor's arse.'

'Well, someone didn't. We need to find out who knew Professor Baird would be standing on that spot, on that day, and at that time.'

'Were there many witnesses?' asks Jenny, eager to begin.

'Around thirty people were seated to hear him speak. They all witnessed the guy being crushed to death but no one could see anything happening on the floor above. And it was an Open Day so there may have been other people milling about elsewhere in the building.'

Alistair offers his first thoughts. 'So that means it could have been anybody.'

'Yes, "Anybody" is our prime suspect so the first thing we need to establish is who didn't like the guy, whether they had a motive to kill him, and their whereabouts at 1 p.m. on Saturday 15th April. Access his phone records, medical records, bank accounts or insurance policies he may have. Jamal, put those hacking skills to good use.'

Jamal, or Techie Jamal as he is known, aged twenty-six, is already legendary in the force for his incredible IT skills. With a degree in Artificial Intelligence he is undoubtedly brilliant, but his communication skills let him down which explains why Jenny and he make such a good pairing.

'We should find out whose idea it was to go there in the first place,' Jenny interrupted, unable to contain her enthusiasm.

'Yes, Jenny, and who knew he'd be giving his lecture from that spot? It looks like the concrete had been moved there prior to the outing. Also find out if there any cctv cameras in the area. With four thousand in Scotland there must be something relevant recorded somewhere.'

Alistair rightly points out, 'The bus driver could have done it.'

'Yes, find out if he has an alibi. Now, I don't know about all of you but I'm hungry. Anyone willing to pop down to the canteen and buy me a bacon and potato scone roll?'

'I'll go," offers Jenny.

'Thanks, Jenny. Now, get to it!'

*

As Alistair drives their new Volkswagen Passat, bought at a good price since the emissions scandal, across the Kingston Bridge, DI Gunn holds up her iPhone and speed reads various articles and tributes paid to Professor Baird.

'Listen to some of these Alistair. The First Minister tweeted: *Extremely sad to hear of the death of the renowned architect Professor Baird.* The President of the Royal Institute of Scottish Architects tweeted: *Honoured to have known such a wonderful architect and educator.* The Minister for Culture tweeted: *Prof Baird was an enormous talent and shall be sadly missed. R.I.P.* What a lot of drivel. Do these people not have work to do Alistair? I wish I had time to sit around tweeting when every Tom, Dick or Harry dies.'

It was taking longer than normal to drive into the city centre from the south side, which made Lorna wonder if leaving Pitt Street had been such a great idea after all.

'I still can't find the cruise control,' complains Alistair. 'I'm going to have to give up and read the manual.'

'If all else fails, read the manual.' Lorna laughs at her own joke and wonders what nonsense people might trot out on hearing of her own demise.

'Who do you want to speak to first at the architecture school?' asks Alistair, pleased he has figured out how to heat his seat.

'Stuart Milne. He's second in command and possibly has the most to gain now the top job is vacant.'

'Can you imagine hating your boss so much you'd want to kill him?'

Lorna narrows her eyes and smiles, 'No, can you?'

Alistair reverses into a tight space in Rose Street.

'Impressive. I doubt I could have manoeuvered my little Fiat into this space.'

The car is parked directly opposite the Glasgow Film Theatre. Lorna, on seeing her favourite haunt, mutters,

'Haven't been there in a while, more's the pity.'

'I've never been, but since the kids were born Susie and I hardly ever go to the cinema.' Alistair bounces out of the car. Everything he does is fast. 'But if we do go we prefer the out-of-town ones. Much easier to get parked.'

Lorna closes her eyes, places the palm of her hand on her chest and takes a deep breath. 'I find that upsetting. Possibly more upsetting than this chap's murder.'

'Don't exaggerate.'

'So you like watching crap American movies, Alistair.'

'Yeh. I can't stand "arty farty" ones. Too slow. Nothing happens.'

'Ye mean realistic ones. Well, Alistair, if that wonderful building ever closes its doors I'll know who to blame. And for the next hour I'd try to keep your opinions about "arty farty" things to yourself'.

They stride up the hill towards the architecture school. They find it hidden among several tall, bland university buildings. It turns out to be far uglier than any of the others. DI Gunn and DC Boyle enter through the heavy steel door which, on closing, makes a clinking sound more familiar in a prison. Inside they face a lift and to the right of it a wide staircase. Lorna automatically presses the button to call the lift as Alistair heads for the stairs.

'Come on. The office is on the first floor.'

Reluctantly, Lorna follows him and, taking in the drabness of the exposed concrete stairwell, complains, 'This building is even worse on the inside.'

'It's not too bad.'

'I might have known you'd like it.'

DI Gunn and DC Boyle exit the stairwell and proceed along a long, bleak corridor towards a sign signaling 'office'. Inside, the name and position of each staff member is displayed under their corresponding, grinning mug shot. A small bell is fastened to the service counter inviting someone to ring it.

Alistair asks, 'Shall I ring the bell?' He rings it before Lorna has a chance to answer.

Seconds later an attractive, busty woman in her forties appears.

'Can I help you?'

Showing her police identification Lorna states, 'Yes, I'm DI Gunn and this is DC Boyle. Would it be possible to have a word with Stuart Milne?'

'Not at the minute I'm afraid. He's interviewing a wannabe architecture student. The poor sod.'

Lorna is taken aback by her forthright views. 'When might he be free?'

She glances at the clock. 'He should be finished in around ten minutes if you want to wait.'

'We'll wait. We'd like to ask you a few questions too if it's okay?'

'Sure.'

Alistair leans in. 'Name?'

'Ms McGovern. Claire McGovern.'

'Ms McGovern, do you know whose idea it was to arrange an outing to the abandoned building?'

Amusement shows in the woman's face. 'That "abandoned building" is an architectural masterpiece, don't you know? And the cinema foyer area, where Professor Baird died, "is an elusive radiance of beauty". We're the plebs who aren't educated enough to appreciate it.'

'What's your own opinion of the building?' asks DI Gunn, egging her on.

'Since you're an officer of the law and I am obliged to tell the truth, I think it is utterly hideous. Always was an eyesore, even when it was in use. Why do you think it shut down after only twelve years?'

Lorna answers, 'Because people started travelling abroad?'

Ms McGovern ignores her and continues, 'The holidaymakers hated it. The locals hated it. The company who commissioned it hated it. I hated it.'

'What else do you hate, Ms McGovern?'

'Well, I hate working here but there's not a lot I can do about that now.'

'Why not?'

'Been here fifteen years. Leaving would muck up my pension and… better the devil ye know.'

'And was Professor Baird a bit of a devil?'

'Oh, yeh. A total big-head. Thought he was God. I suppose in some ways he was.'

'What do you mean?' asks Alistair.

'Well, he had the power to make or break people's careers, didn't he?'

DI Gunn prefers to focus on facts. 'Weren't you required to go on the outing, Ms McGovern?'

'No, but Bernard Hughes, our very own risk-averse Health and Safety Officer, was needed. Right from the outset Bernard said the idea was bonkers.' She shrugs her shoulders. 'And he's been proved right.'

'Ms McGovern. Where were you last Saturday at one p.m.?'

'Saturday? Let me think... Oh yeh, I remember. I was at an all-day meditation workshop at a convent in Schoenstatt.'

'In Germany?'

Ms McGovern smiles for the first time. 'No, it's in the Campsie Fells. It's in a stunning location. Perfect for coping with working here.'

Alistair asks, 'How do ye spell that?'

'C, a, m, p ...'

'No, the other name.'

'Oh, Schoenstatt? I think it's S, c, h, o, e, n, s, t, a, double t.'

They hear light, fast footsteps in the corridor reducing in volume.

'That'll be him free now. I'll let Mr Milne know you're here.'

She picks up the telephone receiver.

'Stuart. That's police detectives here to see you. Shall I send them along?'

They enter a stylishly furnished room with a tremendous view over Glasgow.

'Please, take a seat.'

'Thank you for seeing us, Mr Milne.'

Stuart Milne returns to the comfort of his Bauhaus-inspired chair.

'I'm happy to help in any way I can. It was such a tragic accident. And I feel partly responsible.'

Alistair, notebook at the ready asks, 'Why's that?'

'Well. It was Richard's idea to arrange the site visit to the Clydeview Resort but I should have been more forceful when I tried to talk him out of it. It was foolish. The Health and Safety Officer thought so too.'

'Yes, he said so in his statement after it happened. Is that the reason you didn't go yourself?'

'No, I didn't go because my daughter was getting married.' He adds sarcastically, 'I couldn't get out of that one.'

'Where did she get married?' asks Lorna purely out of nosiness.

'The St Andrew's Church in the Square. It's close to Glasgow Cross. The reception was held there too.'

'Nice. Mr Milne, did you get along with your colleague?'

'What is this? Surely you don't suspect me of anything?'

Lorna replies, 'Mr Milne, we have an idea Professor Baird was murdered.'

'Murdered? My God!'

'Mr Milne, did you like your colleague?'

'Well. I don't want to lie to you and say he was my favourite colleague, but he was a good architect.'

'Did he have a good relationship with his wife?'

Stuart Milne is affronted, 'I have no idea. You'll need to ask her.'

Lorna pushes further, 'Since he spent so much time here, did he ever become especially close to any of his colleagues or students?'

'I don't like what you are insinuating. For goodness' sake, his daughter is in her thirties. And it wouldn't have been possible to have an affair with any of the architectural tutors – unless he was gay or bisexual and I doubt that very much.'

'What? There are no female tutors or lecturers?' Lorna's anger rises. Recently, she attended an event at the Glasgow Women's Library and had been maddened to find out there exists, in Glasgow, only three statues commemorating women and one of those is of Queen Victoria, the woman who spent decades dressed in black mourning the loss of her man.

Stuart Milne tries to backtrack. 'Oh, wait a minute… I believe a young woman was recently temporarily employed to teach Sustainable Architecture. And to answer fully your earlier unpleasant question, as far as I am aware there was only one person Professor Baird ever had an affair with; it was a long one, but it ended several years ago.'

Alistair asks, 'And who was that with?'

'I believe you've just been talking to her.'

Rising from a hard chair, Lorna thanks Stuart Milne for his co-operation and adds, 'Do you think you'll apply for the top job when it's advertised?'

With a haughty air he replies, 'At present, I have no plans to submit an application.'

DI Gunn and DC Boyle weave their way through five studios, one for each year of study, to gain a sense of the general atmosphere of the school. Each studio space is filled with young people sitting at drawing boards, or down on their hands and knees making a hell of a mess trying to build models out of balsa wood or cardboard. Some stand around chatting. One girl is crying. Lorna, speaking in her kindest voice, asks, 'Excuse me, what's wrong?'

The girl blurts out, hysterically, 'I was told to start all over again.'

'Start what again?' asks Lorna, now intrigued.

'Designing an opera house. I can't design another one.' The girl continues crying into a boy's shoulder.

'Why not?'

'The final hand-in is in one month.'

'Who didn't like your design?' Lorna coaxes.

'All of them.' DI Gunn forms the obvious conclusion that 'all of them' must be right.

In the third year studio Alistair spots a pile of sleeping bags. 'Do yez sleep here too?'

'Yeh. When we do all-nighters.'

As DI Gunn and DC Boyle retrace their steps back down the concrete staircase, Alistair points out, 'But doesn't an all-nighter involve staying up all night?'

'I would have thought so.'

Laughing, Alistair asks, 'So why would they need sleeping bags?'

On exiting the building they pass a fresh-faced girl in her late teens being embraced by a woman in her mid-forties, most likely her mother. The mother calls after her 'Good luck!' as the girl, carrying a large, black portfolio case disappears into the architecture school.

The air overhead darkens, signaling rain.

'I'm glad my own daughter has decided not to study architecture,' says Lorna speeding up her pace.

'What? Daisy thought about it?' Alistair is two paces ahead.

'Oh, yeh. When she was little she loved drawing buildings and playing with Lego. We were sure she'd become an architect but a boyfriend got her into computing and now she tells me she wants to go to Dundee to study games programming. She's never away from the computer, unless, of course, she's at a party.'

'Imagine wanting to go there.' Alistair can't understand anyone wanting to leave Glasgow. The rain which has up until now merely been threatening comes down in torrents.

'Dundee's all right. Doesn't rain as much.' They run down the hill towards the car; a race easily won by DC Boyle.

'It doesn't come across as a healthy place to study,' Lorna says as she clicks her seatbelt into place.

'And where are they all gonna get jobs?'

'They could always emigrate.'

Alistair nudges a lever to indicate he's pulling out. 'The secretary's quite bitter, isn't she?'

'Yep. Professor Baird probably promised to leave his wife and didn't. We'll need to interview her again at some point. No doubt about it.'

'Interesting she mentioned the exact spot in the foyer where he died, boss.'

'So she did. But how would Claire McGovern benefit from his death? And if the affair ended a long time ago surely her anger would have subsided by now.'

'Ye'd have thought so, but some women bear grudges forever, don't they?'

'I'm glad you said "some women". C'mon, we need to head back to the station.'

DI Gunn sits at her own uninspiring desk wading through the lengthy document she has received from the forensics lab and, much to her annoyance, a long email sent to her by Techie Jamal. She gleans the relevant points from the forensic report and jots them down in an old-fashioned, lined note pad. Alistair enters carrying two cups of coffee.

'A small cappuccino. Am I right?'

'Yes, thank you. The diet must start today.' Alistair, aware of her extraordinary lack of willpower, rolls his amused eyes and takes a seat opposite.

'Alistair, you've got to stop Techie Jamal sending all these emails. It's ridiculous. I mean, I can see him through the glass. Why can't he tell me in person?'

'Och, ye know what these techie guys are like.'

'Peculiar.'

'Aye, Jamal is more comfortable communicating with machines than humans. That's why he's single. Well, that and the hair gel.'

'God. I hope my daughter doesn't turn out like him.'

'Doesn't seem likely.'

'I'm going to tell him he's wasting police time typing all this drivel with two fingers. And if he wants to get promotion in my department he'll have to speak to me or I'll have no option but to transfer him to the new cybercrime hub in Edinburgh.'

'Threatening to send him to Edinburgh. Yeh, that should frighten him. So, what are forensics saying?'

'Well, the time of death is recorded as five past one which confirms he died instantly and the cause of death is a fractured skull. There were no fingerprints but the footprint they found up above was freshly imprinted and belongs to a size eight walking boot. So it's unlikely to have been made by a woman. The imprint wasn't too deep so they reckon the wearer couldn't have been more than ten and a half/eleven stone.' Lorna pauses, thinking if only she could get down to that weight again. 'Another trace item found in the upper area was a fleck of blue polystyrene similar to the shoe covers the SOCO officers wear but slightly darker. Oh, and a round, wooden broom handle was found at the bottom close to the body.'

'A broom handle?'

'Yep, and I'm wondering if it was used somehow to move the concrete into position.'

'You've lost me.'

'Well, there were no scrape markings above so a machine or simple building method must have been used… or the murderer had an accomplice.'

Alistair tries to visualise a concrete lintel and a single broom handle. 'How can you move a block of concrete with a broom handle?'

Lorna moves a heavy police handbook forwards and backwards over three round incense sticks spaced at intervals.

'I'll explain later in the incident room when I understand it better myself.'

Alistair asks, 'What's Mandarin saying?' This is their nickname for Detective Chief Inspector Darren Russell which has nothing to do with Mandarin ducks or the official language of China and everything to do with his love of all things orange.

'Not happy. He can't stand "middle-class murders" as he calls them. Prefers straightforward thuggery. In these cases it's obvious who committed the murder – the guy who won the fight.'

'It's not nearly so interesting though, is it boss?'

'Jamal's already found out the Prof's wife is a qualified medical doctor and works now as a hypnotherapist. She's got a private practice in Bearsden.'

'That figures. It's full of bored, wealthy housewives.'

'Alistair. Don't be so ignorant.'

DI Gunn hands him a piece of paper. 'We need to meet her. Can you telephone to make an appointment to see Dr Trudy Lamont? Surprisingly, for someone of her generation, it looks like she never changed her name.'

DI Gunn and DC Boyle saunter along Kirk Street near Bearsden Cross searching for number thirty-two. They spot the smartly dressed widow leaving an Italian restaurant and entering a neighbouring door. Giving her a couple of minutes to go on ahead they follow her through the shiny black door complete with gleaming brass ironmongery and climb a flight of stairs. Modern art covers the walls and Rodin's angular, bronze sculpture of *The Thinker* is housed in a glass case on a turn on the stair.

On entering the interior it is evident Trudy Lamont has been greatly influenced by her husband's line of work. While not a big space, it's obvious a huge amount of money has been spent creating this glass, chrome and wood interior softened only by the leather on the chairs and a peace lily plant in the corner. First impressions suggest Dr Trudy Lamont's business is doing fine.

The sprightly widow has already disappeared into a private room beyond the reception area. A young man with wispy dark-blonde hair wearing a crisp, well-ironed shirt which could easily have been purchased from the Ted Baker shop in Princes Square, stops bashing keys on a mobile phone and looks up to see two plain-clothed police officers flashing their ID.

Instantly dropping his cheerful demeanour he asks, 'Have you come to see Dr Dr Lamont?'

Suspecting he has a stutter, DI Gunn confirms, 'Yes, we already have an appointment with Doctor

Lamont.'

'No, it's Dr Dr Lamont.' Both detectives furrow their eyebrows and focus on the receptionist, who right now isn't making much sense.

'She was already a doctor, then she got a PhD,' he explains, smiling.

DI Gunn, irritation rising inside asks, 'Is the brilliant woman free?'

'I'll let her know you're here. Please take a seat.'

As he informs his employer of their presence, Lorna whispers to Alistair, 'She sounds almost as big-headed as the husband.'

Calum gesticulates towards Trudy Lamont's office, 'She says to go through.'

'Thank you for seeing us. I'm Detective Inspector Gunn.'

'Pleased to meet you, Inspector.' Trudy Lamont offers her soft, graceful, beautifully manicured hand.

'I'm Detective Constable Boyle.'

This time offering her hand to Alistair, 'Pleased to meet you, too. Please take a seat.'

Trudy Lamont sits down behind a large oak desk slumping into a luxurious high-backed tan leather Charles Eames chair.

'Dr Dr Lamont, we're dealing with your late husband's case,' explains DI Gunn.

'Please call me Trudy.'

'Thank you.' DI Gunn's eyes are drawn to a professionally taken family portrait on the wall showing four happy faces, 'Have you two children, Trudy?'

'Yes, Jennifer and Charles, all grown up now sadly.' She turns to look at the portrait, 'Seems like only yesterday. Goodness, Charles is nearly forty and Jennifer turned thirty-five last month.' The placid expression on her face falls, her mouth turns downwards.

'I'm so glad Richard was still here for her special party at The House for an Art Lover.' Trudy places her elbows on the table and covers her eyes with her hands and sighs deeply. 'Oh, I'm sorry.' She reaches for her crocodile skin handbag to extract a handkerchief.

DI Gunn opts to play the softly, softly game but with twenty years on the force and a teenage daughter she is no stranger to tears being used to manipulate.

Alistair asks, 'Do your children live locally?'

Trudy's voice is weak, 'Jennifer is here in Glasgow, but Charles lives in London. He's working at Richard's architectural firm in London.

Alistair says, 'Did your late husband have a practice in London, too?'

This generates a slight upturning of her lips. 'No, he works in Richard Roger's practice in London. Richard is a good friend. Have you never heard of him?'

'No.'

'Charles is travelling up today for the funeral on Friday. He's distraught at the death of his father.

We all are, but they were especially close. Had so much in common. Used to visit all the National Trust properties together. I still have Charles' sketchbook from when...'

DI Gunn has heard enough. 'Trudy, we need to know if your husband had any enemies.'

'What are you getting at, Inspector? Surely, it was an accident. I told him the outing was a stupid idea. One of his most stupid. Those horrid buildings are not safe. If they had been demolished long ago when they should have been, this would never have happened.'

DI Gunn lowering and slowing her voice delivers the bombshell, 'Trudy, we have reason to believe your husband was murdered.'

A small scream leaves Trudy's Lancôme-covered lips, her forehead turns into a bar of music without the notes. Shaking her head she blurts out,

'But everyone loved Richard. You'll see if you come to his funeral. Who would want to kill him?'

DI Gunn says, 'Often with that level of success, jealousy follows.'

'Oh I know, Inspector. I know.'

Alistair asks, 'Had there been any unpleasantness between your husband and any of his peers?'

Trudy continues to shakes her head.

'Stuart Milne, for example.'

'They weren't great friends, but no, no nastiness as far as I know. There's only one thing that comes to mind...'

DI Gunn's stomach rumbles, 'And that is?' She imagines the Italian delicacies being served up next door.

'Richard did receive an unpleasant phone call at home recently.'

'Do you know who from?' asks Alistair with his notebook at the ready.

'Ciaran somebody. An architect. He wasn't happy about Richard sitting on the judging panel for the luxury spa commission at Holyrood. But Richard always sat on the judging panels. I don't know what his problem was.'

'Was your husband upset by the call?' Alistair's thoughts turn to the line of hot mince pies in the bakers he spotted round the corner.

'Not especially. He told me he'd also received an unpleasant email from the guy which he'd chosen to ignore. You don't think...?'

'Was he threatened?' asks DI Gunn.

'I don't know, but Richard was a bit upset afterwards.'

'At the time did he inform the police?'

'No, he promised he would if the guy bothered him again, but I don't think he did.'

'Do you know where the architect who phoned him works?'

'Haven't a clue.'

'Okay. That's us done. Unfortunately, the funeral will have to be postponed until the Coroner authorises release of the body. Did your husband wish to be buried or cremated?'

'"For the sake of history, I'd like to be buried," is what he used to say. He left designs for a gravestone, similar to the one in the Necropolis designed by Charles Rennie Mackintosh for Alexander McCall – one of your lot. Richard even scribed the epitaph he wants engraving which I'm in the process of commissioning.'

DI Gunn softened her tone, 'I'm sorry to have to ask this Trudy, but did your husband leave a will?'

'He did.'

'Would it be possible for us to see it?'

'I've nothing to hide. It just so happens I have a copy here in my handbag.'

Trudy picks up her bag from the floor and rummages for the document.

'So many people have asked to see it.' She hands it over. 'Ask my secretary to photocopy it for you if you like.'

The two detectives stand up. 'We'd like to interview your daughter. Could you give us her address, please?' Alistair pulls out his notepad again.

'She lives at 1 Thomson Street, Strathbungo – the first house in the Greek Thomson terrace.'

'The what?'

'Don't tell me you haven't heard of Alexander Greek Thomson, Inspector?'

'I have,' answers DI Gunn as if she were taking part in a quiz. Turning to Alistair, 'He's Glasgow's other famous architect.'

Trudy's eyes and her facial expression show pain. 'It was thanks to my husband Holmwood House was restored to its former glory and is now open to the public. He did so much to preserve our architectural heritage.'

'Sounds worth a visit. Well, thank you for seeing us Trudy. You have been most cooperative.' The two detectives stand up indicating they are ready to leave.

'Just one more thing.' DI Gunn indulges herself by using the classic line from *Columbo*.

'Yes?'

'The sculpture on the stairs. It looks identical to the one in the Burrell Collection.'

'Ah yes, Inspector. Very observant. What most people don't realise is that many castings were made. Rodin's studio produced around eighty copies of the sculpture which was originally called *The Poet*. I love it, don't you?'

*

DI Gunn scans the will as Alistair drives down Nithsdale Road heading for Strathbungo.

'Well, there are no surprises here. It's what you'd expect although the amounts are what I would call... large. He's leaving...' Lorna raises her voice to add emphasis, 'two hundred and fifty thousand each to Charles and Jennifer. Everything else has been left to his wife.'

'Two hundred and fifty grand!'

'I know. When you think of all the food banks in Glasgow,' DI Gunn laments.

'Even I would consider bumping off someone for that.'

'Well, there's one thing I can say about this family, they have good taste,' DI Gunn concedes as she and Alistair walk up the path to the exquisite home of Dr Jennifer Baird.

Lorna presses the doorbell set in an Egyptian relief carving. They hear the sounds of small children chasing around the hall. 'Sounds like someone's home.'

The door opens to reveal a fit, young woman wearing torn jeans with nails painted electric blue to match her seductive, smoky eye make-up. In one arm she holds a chubby, blue-eyed baby. Behind them an opulent mahogany carved staircase flows up from a marble-tiled floor lit at the top by a fabulous, original skylight.

Alistair wasn't expecting someone quite so attractive, 'Dr Jennifer Baird?'

'Afraid not. I'm the nanny. She's at work.'

DI Gunn shows her ID. 'It's nothing to worry about. We want to talk to her about what happened to her father.'

'Oh, isn't it so sad? Jennifer says the whole city's in mourning.'

Lorna doubts there is a great deal of mourning going on in Possilpark, Easterhouse and places of that ilk. Aware of the baby wrestling in the young woman's arms she asks,

'And where might Jennifer Baird work?'

'Up at the Glasgow School of Art. Dr Baird is a Lecturer in Art History.'

'Well, sorry to have disturbed you, Ms?'

'Poplawski. Celina Poplawski.' Alistair jots it down as she spells it out. 'And I think we detectives know how to find the Glasgow School of Art.'

*

Arriving at 167 Renfrew Street, DI Gunn and DC Boyle enter through the left of two solid black swing doors. Passing in the opposite direction, coming out through the 'OUT' door, are young, scruffily dressed students covered in paint.

Lorna and Alistair head for the office where they introduce themselves and wait to be collected by Richard Baird's daughter.

'My office is on the top floor and there's no lift I'm afraid. I hope you're fit.'

'Fighting,' lies Lorna.

Jennifer Baird, a slim, fit woman in her mid-thirties, leads them up the first flight of stairs through a double height museum space which Jennifer informs them 'is currently exhibiting Japanese art' and on up three more flights.

At the top, Dr Baird pushes through a door housing a stained glass rose motif.

DI Gunn looks back at the stain glass, 'The roses are a nice touch.'

Jennifer slows her walking pace, 'Mackintosh said, "*Art is the Flower. Life is the Green Leaf. Let every artist strive to make his flower a beautiful living thing, something that will convince the world that there may be, there are, things more precious more beautiful – more lasting than life itself.*"'

They continue along a long, glazed south-facing corridor taking in the superb aerial view of the city.

'This is what is affectionately known as the "hen run". My office is through here on the right.'

DI Gunn and DC Boyle sit in hard, wooden high back chairs designed to ensure the occupants don't outstay their welcome. They could easily have been created by Charles Rennie Mackintosh. Jennifer Baird sits facing them settling into a plush Danish-designed office chair covered in purple fabric. Art nouveau framed tapestries and ink drawings adorn the walls. They match the furniture perfectly.

DI Gunn, in a sympathetic voice, says, 'We're sorry we have to question you at this time Dr Baird.'

'You can't upset me any more than I am already. Who'd want to hurt my father? Everyone loved him.'

'So, you've already spoken with your mother?'

'Yes, she called me straight after you left. As you can imagine she's as distraught as I am, but I can't imagine how I can help you.'

'We never know what little piece of information might trigger a new line of enquiry,' Alistair explains. 'Sometimes we find the murderer by a process of elimination and not the other way round.'

'You didn't go on the outing to the resort,' states DI Gunn.

'Only because I'd been there before, several times, in the past with Dad.'

'How old were you?'

'About nine or ten.' Jennifer's face strains at the recollection.

'Are you aware of any favourite areas your father had within the cinema building?'

'Oh yes. He was most proud of the foyer space. He designed the area so beautifully allowing light to filter in through the small windows punctured at intervals in the solid west wall.'

This is the wrong answer.

DI Gunn asks, 'Where were you at one p.m. on Saturday 8th April?'

'What are you suggesting, Inspector?'

'Please answer the question, Dr Baird.'

'Ehmm, I was probably at home with my children.'

'I'm afraid probably isn't good enough. Could anyone vouch for that?'

Jennifer Baird covers her face with her hands, 'I've just lost my father and you ask me these monstrous questions. You wouldn't if you knew how close we were. I loved my father.'

DI Gunn has heard enough. 'I realise this is difficult for you Dr Baird, but we need to know in order to eliminate you from our enquiries. You are, after all, a significant benefactor in your father's will.'

Pretending to cry, Jennifer mumbles, 'You think I care about money?'

'Please tell us your whereabouts.' Alistair is hoping to finish early to head up to the golf course to practice his chipping.

Finally, Dr Baird reaches for and flicks through a large art nouveau fabric covered desk diary and places a thin piece of gold ribbon to mark the correct page.

'That day I went running with my friends Sophie and Claire. I'm training for a half-marathon to raise money for the *Mackintosh Fire Appeal*.'

Lorna responds, 'I'm running a 5k race to raise money towards having a Mary Barbour statue erected in Govan.'

Jennifer screws up her nose. 'Who?'

'She was a councillor and political activist who led the Glasgow rent strikes of 1915.'

'Oh, how interesting.'

Alistair is losing patience. 'Where and at what time did you go running?'

'We met at the gates of Bellahouston Park at ten thirty.'

'Do you know how long you were running?'

Referring again to her diary she replies, 'I've written here we ran for one hour and met up again at one thirty in a brasserie in Shawlands. It was Claire's birthday, you see.'

Alistair places a piece of paper and a pen in front of her. 'Could you please write down the names and addresses of your friends?'

'What did you do in between those times?' asks DI Gunn.

'I popped home to get cleaned up.'

'Was your husband looking after the children?'

'No, he plays tennis at the Titwood Tennis Club on Saturday mornings. Celina, whom you've met already, would have been watching them.'

DI Gunn rises stiffly from the chair.

'There are a lot of doctors in your family, aren't there?'

'Only my mother and myself. Dad doesn't even have a degree, but it was the way in his day. It didn't stop him being a genius.'

DI Gunn and DC Doyle exit the Glasgow School of Art and negotiate the main steps. They walk past several students busy smoking and gossiping.

'Alistair, do you think you could grab us a sandwich from Marks and Sparks? I'll meet you back at the car. I want to pop into the architecture department again to see Claire McGovern. See if I can get any info on students who might bear a grudge against the high heid yin.'

'Okay boss. What d'you want?'

'Get me any filling, I'm not fussed.'

Alistair takes off down the hill and enters the back door of Mark & Spencer, promising a Big Issue vendor he'll buy a magazine on the way out.

*

Claire McGovern sits at her desk eating a lean chicken salad from a Tupperware box. When she sees DI Gunn she puts a lid on the tub and puts it to one side.

'Back so soon, Inspector?'

Lorna approaches the counter. 'I was wondering, Ms McGovern?'

'Yes?'

'I was wandering why you referred to the person being interviewed for entry to your school as "a poor sod"'.

Claire's eyes reduce to a slant. 'Because, Inspector, this course isn't what they expect it to be.'

DI Gunn replies, 'What? Isn't it enjoyable?'

'Well they enjoy the first few weeks but within a few months they are usually experiencing problems. Because the truth is the course is hugely subjective. Everyone knows it, but no one ever admits it. We're all supposed to keep up the pretence. Some days I feel like I'm acting a part in *The Emperor's New Clothes*, but, unlike in the fairy tale, no one ever points out the obvious.'

DI Gunn's sympathetic facial expressions encourage Claire McGovern to continue. She is on a roll.

'The students become more and more anxious as the course progresses and by fifth year they are nervous wrecks. I'm not kidding, I'm like an informal counsellor.'

'Really?'

'Students are expected to work on their projects in the studios twenty-four seven. They survive on a diet of junk food and drugs.' She lowers her voice, 'Not all of them legal.'

'Sounds awful.'

'My heart bleeds for them.' She shakes her head. 'It's not right.'

'Ms McGovern, could you give me the names of any students who are having difficulty right now and a list of students who have been failed as far back as you can, please?'

'I've only got records going back ten years.'

'Ten years is fine.' DI Gunn hands her a card. 'Can you email them to me?'

'Yeh, sure and I think you'll find the figures are… criminal.'

*

DI Gunn wipes the information she no longer considers relevant from a whiteboard and replaces it with newly acquired information and photographs which have recently come in from forensics.

She flips over a page of a sketch pad to reveal a drawing of a concrete lintel resting on three round pieces of wood, or broom handles, positioned next to a hole.

'That's good. Did you do it yourself?' Jamal studies the drawing.

'Yes,' Lorna responds, proudly.

'I thought it was easier to understand if I showed you a drawing.'

Alistair enters talking on his mobile phone, 'I've booked a tee time for one p.m. on Sunday.'

DI Gunn coughs, 'Oh, excuse me, Alistair. Am I interrupting something?'

Alistair cuts the call short.

'Sorry, boss, but it's the club championship. I'm through to the quarter-final.'

'Congratulations. Now if we can focus for now on this enquiry.'

Lorna points at the round broom handles. 'These round pieces of wood reduce friction so allowing the concrete block to be pushed easily along the ground.'

She pauses to let the information sink in.

'But if you push it forward, wouldn't the block eventually roll off the back pole?' Jenny queries.

'Yes, you're right but the back pole can be inserted again at the front to continue rolling the concrete.'

Jamal says, 'But you'd still need strength to lift the concrete up to insert the poles underneath, wouldn't you?'

'Not necessarily.' Lorna reveals another competent drawing showing how a plank of wood with a wedge-shaped end could be used as a lever to lift the block of concrete up at one end.

'With an item placed in the middle underneath to balance it, the lever can operate like a see-saw. Then you step on the end of the plank and, hey presto, the end of the concrete is lifted up. Isn't it clever... and so simple?'

Her young team nod in unison.

'After the concrete lintel was moved to the edge of the hole, the lever was positioned under this end of the lintel ready to be tipped up.'

'Did you work out all this yerself?' asks Alistair.

'No, but I have my sources.' Lorna smiles as she taps, with her forefinger, the side of her nose.

'Pure dead brilliant,' replies Alistair.

'Well, now we know how it was done and that the technique requires little strength, we need to find out who else had a motive to kill him, male or female. Jamal, you were to find out the extent of Richard Baird's wealth.' She looks directly at Jamal, 'But I want you to talk to me. I don't want to receive any more of these essay type emails. You're not at university anymore.'

Jamal's eyes display terror as he grudgingly removes them from his computer screen. He picks up a printed sheet of paper and turns to face his senior.

'Professor Baird had a salary of £85,000 plus bonus if he generated fees over a certain amount from overseas students which he usually achieved. His architectural practice last year made profits of £1.1 million of which he received £250,000 and he earned roughly £14,000 from giving outside lectures and after dinner speeches.'

DI Gunn shakes her head and sighs, 'His talks aren't even interesting. And what do I get for entertaining you lot? I get to keep my job.' She pauses for effect. 'But was he a big spender?'

'No,' continues Jamal, 'his many savings accounts and shares amounted to over a million.'

'So, the widow of Richard Baird will inherit a tidy sum.'

Alistair reminds her, 'But his wife couldn't have done it. She was sitting in the audience looking straight at him.'

DI Gunn despairs, 'As were all his colleagues except Stuart Milne, number two up at the architecture school, but his alibi checks out. And the snooty daughter's alibi stands up too. Her friends confirmed she went running with them late morning and a waiter in the brasserie in Shawlands remembers them being loud, ordering several bottles of champagne and leaving a lousy tip. And we are dealing with one of those rare families which claims to get on swimmingly, love each other unconditionally and never argue. I don't know about you but I find that deeply suspicious.'

DI Gunn paces from one side of the whiteboard to the other.

Alistair asks, 'Did you remember to ask Claire McGovern her shoe size?'

'Oh, damn it! No, I didn't. But there's a ninety-nine percent chance it's less than a size eight although she could have been wearing bigger boots and thick socks. We can only rule out anyone larger than an eight.'

Alistair reminds her, 'Claire McGovern did mention the cinema foyer spot being especially significant.'

'True. Well remembered.'

Jenny can't stay silent any longer, 'The son, Charles, also benefits financially from his father's death.'

'I've arranged access to his mobile phone records,' confirms Jamal. 'If he made a call that day in the London area, that'll verify where he was.'

'Good, Jamal, now the two of you, I want you to check out the alibi of a Claire McGovern. She claims to have been at an all-day meditation workshop somewhere near Lennoxtown. Alistair will give you the exact details.'

Alistair rips out the page from his notebook.

DI Gunn continues, 'The wife told us her husband received a nasty email followed by a threatening phone call about two weeks ago from an architect working in Glasgow. His name is Ciaran, that's all she could tell us. But I'm sure you techie kids'll be able to track down the email.'

'Yes, boss.' Jamal smooths down his shiny black hair. 'I could do a search for the name Ciaran in the body of the email right now if you want?'

'Can you do that?'

'Yes.' Jamal is baffled at how computer illiterate his boss is. He recalls a funny argument with her once in the pub when she was adamant that the old floppy disks she used were not floppy.

'Will it take long, Jamal?'

'Ten seconds.'

Jamal returns to his preferred position in front of a computer screen. He hits a few keys on the keyboard and scrolls down by repeatedly tapping the 'down' key. Jamal's views are harsh when it comes to computing; he believes 'only losers use a mouse'.

Jamal's eyes are glued to the screen. 'He received an email from a Ciaran Wilson on 15th March.'

'Good. What's it say?'

Scrolling down some more, he replies, 'It's quite long.'

Jenny, already peering over his shoulder says, 'I'll read it.'

Professor Baird,

When the most lucrative architectural contracts in Scotland are up for grabs, I notice you ALWAYS choose the designs of your former pupils. You loved Edwin Jones public toilet inspired design, did you? The hellish concrete block my four-year-old son could have drawn. You preferred it to my firm's fabulous glass and steel design, did you? Well I don't believe you can be THAT BLIND.

Since the undeserving winner for the Luxurious Spa was announced three weeks ago I have discovered you are Godparent to Edwin Jones's son and last summer you holidayed on his uncle's yacht in Cannes. How cosy. How crooked. Ever heard of CONFLICT OF INTEREST Professor Baird?

You must enjoy watching architectural firms in Scotland going under while yours thrives. Well I've written to my member of parliament demanding a public enquiry and I'm holding you personally responsible for the collapse of my firm.

Yours sincerely
Ciaran Wilson BSc BArch RISA

'Punchy...'

'The url is wilsongrantarchitects.' Jamal types this into a search engine and clicks on maps. 'The firm's address is Brunswick Street in the Merchant City.'

'Ten out of ten, Jamal. At last we have a suspect with a motive. And this guy does sound pretty deranged.'

*

DI Gunn and DC Boyle peer into the window of an office unit in Brunswick Street.

'It looks like they've packed up.' Alistair fishes his mobile phone out of his trouser pocket. 'We could try calling. I've already put the number in my phone.'

'Well done, you. Yes, go ahead, try it.'

Alistair, with the speed of Techie Jamal, calls the number. He hears a dial tone to suggest the number still exists.

'Hello, Ciaran Wilson.'

'Hello, Mr Wilson, this is Detective Constable Alistair Boyle.'

'Oh,' he replies in a deflated fashion.

'We need to ask you a few questions. It's in connection with the death of Professor Richard Baird.'

'Oh, no.'

'Oh, yes. Where can we find you or would you prefer to meet down the station?'

'You'll need to come here. I can't leave my children alone in the house.'

'I hope the handbrake's good.'

Alistair yanks on the brake as far as it goes and puts the car into first gear to ensure it won't roll back down the steep hill. They are in Gardner Street in the district of Partick, a stone's throw from Professor Baird's townhouse in Dowanhill, but a world away in terms of economic status. Ciaran Wilson lives on the ground floor which turns out to be ten steps up from the sloping pavement.

'Come in.' Ciaran holds a smiling, brown-eyed, gurgling, baby girl.

DI Gunn and DC Boyle are led through a cluttered hall, past a bicycle and folded up pram and into the living room.

'I'll put the kids next door, but I won't be able to leave them for too long.' Ciaran speaks with a lyrical northern Irish accent. He's slightly built. Likely no more than eleven stone.

'This shouldn't take long, Mr Wilson.'

The room is furnished with simple, 1970s period furniture; the focal point is a fire place with oak surround and art deco metal inset. Hanging on the walls are framed copies of Charles Rennie Mackintosh's ink drawings. A large bay window houses an Ercol inspired dining table and chairs.

Ciaran enters the room.

Lorna says, 'I love your fireplace.'

'Thanks. We got it from the architectural salvage yard. Is this about the stupid email I sent Professor Baird?'

'Afraid so,' replies Alistair.

'Oh, shit.' Ciaran sits down and stares into the flames of the fire.

'And according to Professor Baird's widow you also made a threatening phone call to his home. Is that true?' Alistair has his notebook at the ready.

'Uh-huh. But I was cracking up at the time.'

'Cracking up? How'd ye mean?'

'Well, my business had gone tits up. I'm waiting to be declared bankrupt. And this "starter flat" which is too small for us is about to be repossessed. We bought it in January 2007, right at the peak of the market. Turns out it was my first minus step on the ladder.'

Lorna interjects, 'But I thought architects are well paid.'

'Everyone thinks that, but people rarely use one. Have either of you ever employed an architect?'

DI Gunn and DC Boyle shake their heads.

'Thought not. Everyone goes to a doctor and dentist and, by the time they are a certain age, an optician, but hardly anyone uses an architect. Yet, the general public think there is some architecture fairy godmother sprinkling cash on us. Well, there isn't.' Ciaran's eyes narrow. 'And that greedy individual took everything going and dictated what the building environment in Scotland should look like. Imagine having that power.' Ciaran's accent becomes more Irish as his anger rises.

'Let's get this clear, Mr Wilson. Are you talking about Professor Baird?'

'Uh-huh. I wasn't the only one to despise him, but I shouldn't have called him at home or sent the email. I was on tilt and had been drinking. It all came to a head. I sent the email because I wasn't expecting to be around to face the music.'

'What d'ye mean?' asks Alistair naively.

'Well, when Professor Baird was on that ridiculous trip to his derelict dump, I was considering throwing myself in the Clyde.'

'What stopped you?' asks Lorna, especially glad now her daughter has decided against at career in architecture.

'I couldn't do it to Olivia.'

'She is?

'My wife. She's an architect too. That's how lucky we are,' Ciaran adds sarcastically.

'Is she working at the moment?'

'Yes, but her contract's about to end.'

'Could anyone corroborate where you were at 1 p.m. on Saturday 15th April?'

'What, you think I killed him?'

'We need to know where you were so we can eliminate you from our enquiries.'

'I was alone.'

'What side of the river were you walking along?' asks Alistair.

'It was the Clyde Street side.'

'Around what time?'

Ciaran's voice rises and quickens, 'I don't know.'

'Roughly?'

'Roughly dinner time.'

'Oh, that can mean different things to different people, Mr Wilson, depending on your class.'

'Oh, I'm definitely working class. It was in the middle of the day. I dunno, roughly two o'clock.'

'Can you remember anything else you did?'

'I spoke to a down-and-out. I've seen him before. He sleeps under Jamaica Bridge.'

'What did he say to you?' asks Lorna, genuinely interested in the advice ministered by a tramp.

'He told me to go ahead and do it.'

Alistair shakes his head and rolls his eyes, 'Charming.'

'And then I went into St Andrew's Cathedral,' recalls Ciaran. 'But I couldn't prove that either.'

'Are you Catholic, Mr Wilson?' asks Alistair, a former pupil of St Mungo's. Despite being an altar boy in his youth, Alistair now only ever ventures into churches to attend weddings and funerals.

Ciaran replies, 'No, I went in to look at the Peter Howson painting.'

'Were you there long?'

'I don't know. I can't remember. Maybe an hour. As I say, I was upset.'

'Well, thank you for answering our questions.' DI Gunn is grateful they now have a lead. 'That's all isn't it, Alistair?'

'Yes, I can't think of anything else.'

On the way out, as Alistair rushes towards the car, Lorna pauses on the doorstep.

'Where will you go?' she asks, concerned for the young family.

'We're lucky. My parents have said we can stay with them until we get back on our feet.'

'Oh, talking of feet. We forgot to ask... What size of shoe do you wear?'

Ciaran throws a puzzled look, 'An eight, why?'

'You're not going.' DI Gunn raises her voice to the phone. 'I don't care who else is going.' Her daughter, at the other end, hangs up.

DI Gunn, seated at her desk, closes her eyes and takes a few deep breaths to recover from yet another argument with her teenage daughter. Is it too much to ask her to stay home the weekend before sitting Higher English? Lorna stands up to pour water from a little green plastic watering can into the earth surrounding her money plant. Jenny pops her head around the door.

'Busy?'

Lorna looks up, 'Oh, it's yourself.'

Jenny smiles as she pushes her chestnut, chin-length hair round her petite ears.

'I thought only Gaelic speakers use that expression.'

'Well, my mother was from Skye but I don't have the Gaelic myself. I wish I did so I could run away to the Isle of Harris and shack up with a strong, handsome Hebridean.'

'But wouldn't your husband and daughter miss you?'

'There's no harm in dreaming Jenny. Have you checked out Claire McGovern's alibi?'

'Yes.'

'And?'

Jenny takes a seat. 'Well, a nun checked her records and confirmed that Claire was there all day, and she recalled how well she sat in the lotus position. The group didn't even leave the building for lunch.'

'Well, that rules her out but she might know something that will unlock the key. She's going to provide me with a list of students who have had major problems within the last ten years. I'll pass them to you and Jamal as soon as they come in. Should be tomorrow.'

'Cool. Do you want anything from the canteen?' asks Jenny, a people pleaser.

'I'm supposed to be on a diet but I don't suppose one little plate of chips'll do any harm.'

'I've heard today's special is macaroni and cheese.'

'Oh, brilliant, in that case get me macaroni cheese and a small amount of chips. Thanks Jenny. I'll get the money.'

'Oh, and after lunch boss, is it okay if Jamal and I head over to the Blythswood Square hotel to ask around there? It's where the awards ceremony was held a few days prior to the murder.'

'Yes of course Jenny. Keep asking questions.'

'We've plenty of them, right enough.'

'The Chief Inspector is already breathing down my neck.'

'Can't he see we're doing our best?'

'No, he can't because he's sunning himself in Majorca. I received a postcard this morning. That's how old-fashioned he is.' Smiling she adds, 'He taken a trip on an orange train.'

Lorna hands Jenny the postcard showing a photograph of a train. Jenny looks confused.

'The train was built to carry oranges across the island. He obviously thinks it's funny.'

Alistair passes the door carrying a putter.

Lorna calls after him, 'Alistair.'

Alistair steps back and pauses at his boss's open door.

'How'd you get on in your golf match?'

'I won seven and six.'

Jenny asks, 'Is that good?'

'I hammered him. That's me through to the semi-final.'

'Well done, you! Have you applied for a warrant yet to search Ciaran Wilson's home?'

'Did it first thing, boss. And I've contacted the priest at St Andrew's Cathedral to ask around.'

'And just so you know, Jenny and Jamal are taking the car for a couple of hours. They're going over to The Blythswood to ask a few questions.'

Alistair turns to Jenny, 'If you find out how the cruise control works let me know.'

*

'You'd be best to talk to Aaron Guthrie.' A pretty young girl behind the swanky bar continues to polish a glass. 'He was probably on that night and he's almost an architect. I'll go and get him.'

'That would be great,' responds Jenny enthusiastically.

A young man with a perfectly messy hairstyle appears from behind the scenes, looking worried when they produce their identity badges.

'Oh, it's nothing to worry about,' soothes Jenny, 'we want to ask some questions about the night all the architects were here.'

'We'd better take a seat.' Aaron ushers them over to a quiet booth. They sit down on the dark Harris Tweed seating.

'Aaron, did you know that Professor Baird's death is being treated as murder?' asks Jamal.

'Yeh, I heard it on the news. I still can't believe it, but I don't see how I can help you.'

'We'd like to know, Aaron, if anyone at the awards ceremony mentioned the outing arranged for the following Saturday, to go to the former Clydeview Holiday Resort?'

'Oh, the president guy announced it.'

'What did he say?'

'He said a bus would be leaving from the architecture department, maybe at midday?'

'That was when the bus left. And was there any mention Professor Baird would be giving a talk from the cinema foyer area?'

'Yeh, he mentioned that too.' Jenny scribbles in her notebook while Jamal takes cryptic notes using a phone app.

Jenny continues, 'The girl behind the bar said you're almost an architect. What did she mean?'

'Well, I've passed RIBA parts one and two, but because I can't get a job in an architect's office I can't get the work experience to be eligible to sit part three.'

Jenny and Jamal, having completed straightforward courses at university, have no idea what he's talking about.

Jenny, never lost for words says, 'Architecture's a long course, isn't it?'

'Yeh, five years full-time but it feels longer.'

'And now you work here?'

'And now I work here.' Aaron repeats like a parrot.

'So many of my friends with Law degrees work in bars too. Ever thought about joining the police?'

Jamal interrupts, 'Did you train at the architecture school in Glasgow?'

'Yes.'

'And did you like Professor Baird?'

'He was no worse than the other tutors, but I thought everyone outside the school loved him... until that night.'

'What do you mean?'

'Well, after the ceremony was over people started drinking way too much and I overheard people dissing him.'

Jenny pulls out a photograph of their main suspect, Ciaran Wilson.

'Do you recognise this man?'

'Eh, maybe. He might have been one of them. I was concentrating on pouring wine without spilling it.'

'What exactly were people saying?' probes Jamal.

'The younger architects were complaining about their jobs,' Aaron lets out a sigh, 'They should try mine... Oh, and I overhead one guy ranting about national design competitions. He claims Professor Baird always selects the designs of his former pupils.'

Aaron looks again at the photo. 'He could have been that guy. He did have similar hair. I was standing up, he was sitting down. I thought it was funny when I overheard him saying he'd be "celebrating the day he snuffs it".'

Jenny looks deadly serious, 'What's funny about that?'

Aaron jolts backwards, 'Obviously, he didn't mean it.'

'How do you know he didn't mean it?'

'Look! I don't want to get the guy into trouble. He was drunk. People say things like that don't they? They don't mean it... literally.'

'Did you overhear anything else significant?' Jamal tries to wrap up the conversation.

'I don't know if it's significant, but I heard some woman complaining the professor is misogynistic.'

'Do you think he treated women unfairly?' Jenny didn't think any profession could be worse than Law.

'Oh, Yeh, I saw it when I was at architecture school, but saying that, they can be nasty to anyone – if your face doesn't fit.'

'Did your face fit, Aaron?'

'I rarely lifted it. I never answered back, always toed the line because if you don't pass the course you can't become an architect. That was my dream since I was about ten years old.' Aaron lets out a little laugh, 'Didn't do me any good though, did it? Got the qualification which almost killed me and now I work here. I've got two degrees in architecture but I still can't call myself an architect.' He looks around the room and sighs.

Looking again at the photograph he says, 'I remember the guy's voice was quite loud. Oh, and he was Irish.'

*

'This is where it gets interesting.' Jamal points at his computer screen which shows the results of a Microsoft Access query.

'How did you do that?' asks Alistair hugely impressed.

'I converted the three spreadsheets DI Gunn was sent from the Office Manager up at the architecture school into a single database. The first spreadsheet includes all the students who were failed at the end of years one, two, three, four or five. The second spreadsheet includes all those who repeated the year and the final result of the repeat year.'

Alistair wishes he hadn't asked. Jamal continues, his face animated,

'And a third spreadsheet shows a list of students who appealed the decision and how long their correspondence continued thereafter. Now I have all the information in the database, I'm able to write queries. The query I have run has returned a list of former students with the greatest reasons to be resentful.'

'Brilliant, Jamal.' Lorna smiles, tucking into her mid-morning crispy bacon roll.

Jamal beams with pride. 'The top of the list, with by far the greatest motive to kill Professor Baird, is a Miss Eva Paterson.'

'What's her profile?'

'She was failed at the end of fifth year, but for some strange reason, even though the university regulations allowed it, she wasn't given an opportunity to re-sit. She repeated the fifth year and was failed again.'

'My God!' DI Gunn is shocked. 'So, in total she'd completed six years full-time at university and never qualified as anything.'

'Not only that, boss.' Jamal is on a roll. 'But she and her family spent five years fighting the decision. They even started a legal challenge.'

'Don't tell me. She wasn't granted legal aid.'

'You guessed it.'

'Well done, Jamal. We need to find out where she is now, what she's doing and, more importantly, where she was on Saturday 15ᵗʰ April at one p.m.' She adds, 'Since you and Jenny seem to be good at extracting information from former students, you two can investigate that lead further while Alistair and I continue to focus on Ciaran Wilson. We'll go down this afternoon to put up a poster in St Andrew's Cathedral. Until we have somehow linked him to the scene of the crime, we need to keep all other lines of enquiry open. Oh, and did anyone check out the alibi of the bus driver?'

Alistair replies, 'I did. His boss confirmed he called the driver from head office via their new radio system and he answered it at 12:58 p.m. So, even at a sprinting pace he couldn't have reached the second floor of the cinema building in six minutes.'

Lorna rolls her eyes, 'Another solid alibi. Did he count how many passengers he had?'

'Yes, twenty-four out and twenty-five on the return journey. The extra one was me.'

DI Gunn points to her whiteboard. 'There were thirty seats lined up here when the professor began his talk. The health and safety guy said there were only four empty seats so twenty-six seats were taken. Who were the other two?'

'The architect's wife came in a taxi,' Alistair reminds her.

'So she did. Any idea who the twenty-sixth was?'

Alistair refers back to the pile of statements taken at the crime scene and his own notes. 'It was a middle-aged woman who came on a service bus from Helensburgh. She was the nurse who pronounced him dead at the scene.'

'Yes, but unlike our own police doctor she wasn't paid for it,' DI Gunn adds bitterly, 'If I'd been paid for every dead body I'd seen in my life I'd be a wealthy woman.'

'Don't you think it's a bit odd her going up to that creepy building by herself?' Jenny isn't the bravest female officer on the force.

'It was an Open Day.'

'Still, she's the odd one out. All the others were connected to the architecture school. Should we at least check her out, boss?'

'Yes, please do. Now, if that's everything I'm meeting a friend for lunch at the *Two Fat Ladies*.'

As they leave the incident room, Jenny adds, cheerily, 'Oh, Alistair. Jamal figured out the cruise control in seconds. Ye flick up the indicator switch and push in the side button.'

*

'Eva Paterson being a fairly unusual name made it easier to track her down. It's a nice name, don't you think?' Jenny happily chats to Jamal as they wander down a dirt track leading to the heart of the Carbeth Hutters community.

'I love getting out the office, don't you?' Jenny breathes in the fresh air and listens to the sounds of birds chirping. 'Oh! Some of these huts are so cute. I'd like to live here.'

'Maybe for a few days in summer. Ye know they've no gas or electricity. Even worse... no wi-fi.'

'I think I'd cope with that better than you. Just saying,' Jenny smirks. 'The huts are nearly all green. What's the name of Eva's hut?'

'The Chalet,' replies Jamal.

'That narrows the search down – not.'

An old man appears, walking towards them with a collie dog in tow. At close range he smiles and says, 'It's a braw day.' This is a very different environment from the harshness of the city where people regard individuals as mad if they so much as smile or say hello.

'Hello,' Jenny smiles, 'do you know where we'd find The Chalet.'

The old man's eyes narrow, he points his index finger at them. 'You'd better not be from the Department of Social Security.'

Jenny replies, 'No… No, we're looking for our friend Eva.'

'Just as well.' The old man's face softens. 'She's had enough hassle from that crowd. Her hut is through there behind the large fern.'

They continue thanking him as they trample on through the mossy woodland. Once past the numerous branches of fern, a modest, green stained hut comes into view. An athletic, good-looking woman with mid-length brown hair flecked with grey, wearing denim dungarees is hanging out washing. When she spots Jamal and Jenny she gently smiles.

'Can I help you?'

Jenny calls out, 'I hope so.'

Up close they produce their police IDs which causes Eva's smile to fall in an instant.

'We need to ask you a few questions about your connection to Professor Baird.'

'What connection?' Eva angrily sticks a peg into the line.

'Did you know he was dead?' asks Jenny.

'No.' She pauses and adds, 'Good.'

'He was only sixty-two.'

Eva angrily sticks a second peg in to secure flowery pyjama bottoms to the clothes line. 'He's had a great life.'

'Eva, are you aware he was murdered?'

'Until you told me, I didn't even know he was dead. I don't read newspapers. I don't have a computer or a television.'

'What about a radio?'

'I've a wind up radio but I never listen to the news propaganda, spouting forth topics of hate to make us more and more fearful so in the end we beg you lot to protect us. All done so we'll give up our civil liberties willingly.'

Jenny notices George Orwell's novel *1984* splayed face down on a wooden stool. 'That's an interesting way of looking at things, Ms Paterson.'

'Look, we hutters have had a terrible time battling the landowner here. The rent strike lasted ten years. It got nasty and my friend actually had his hut torched. Why couldn't you lot have come round then?' Eva stabs in another peg. 'Protect *us* for once instead of doing everything you can to protect the rich and powerful.' She looks directly at Jenny. 'They don't need protecting.'

'You seem pretty angry, Ms Paterson.' Jamal is quick on the uptake.

'I am angry. So would you be. Listen, are you going to be long because I've got to head into Milngavie in an hour to go to work.'

'You've got a job?'

'Yes and no. I work twenty hours a week in a horrid pound shop stacking shelves otherwise they'll stop my Jobseeker's Allowance of £72.40 a week.'

Jenny is shocked and her instinct is always to help. 'We could drop you off if you like. This won't take long.'

Eva picks up the empty basket. 'Look, you'd better come in.'

They enter a sunlit, timber lined room oozing warmth with a wood burning stove in the corner. A chunky open timber staircase leads to a sleeping gallery above. A lithe black cat pads down the stairs to greet them. Eva picks the cat up and strokes her lovingly.

Eva smiles, 'This is Charbon... It's French for coal.' Charbon purrs. 'I collected her from the rescue home on *National Black Cat Day*.'

Jenny reaches out to stroke her. 'Oh! She's lovely.'

Jamal, preferring dogs, becomes impatient. 'We need to know where you were at one p.m. on Saturday 15th April.'

'I don't know.'

'Ms Paterson, we really need to know,' encourages Jenny.

Eva sits down in a wooden rocking chair. 'Please sit down.' Charbon settles on Eva's knee. 'Recently, I'm only ever here at the hut or at the shop in Milngavie. Occasionally, I'm out hill-walking or on my bike at weekends.'

Jenny and Jamal sit side by side on a faded orange, vintage sofa. Jenny spots an old-fashioned mobile phone next to a magazine about sustainable living. She hands Eva a piece of paper with her number at the station. 'Can you find out whether you were working that day and call me?'

'I've never hurt anyone in my entire life and everyone seems to want to hurt me.' Eva's anger has been replaced with self-pity.

'Who else wants to hurt you?'

'Professor Baird. He did everything in his power to hurt me.'

'Do you blame Professor Baird for not becoming an architect?' asks Jenny.

'It was his decision.' Eva folds back the cat's ears as she glides her hand over her smooth, glossy head.

Jenny is interested, 'Did you follow the university appeal's procedure?'

'There is no appeal's procedure against an academic decision. And that is written into every university constitution.' Eva smiles sadly. 'Of course you don't think to read the university rule book before starting first year, do you?' Charbon, now being tickled under the chin, purrs loudly.

Jenny is confused. 'So what is the appeal's procedure for?'

'Students can only appeal on health grounds. They can never, ever, ever have their work reassessed. I know because I tried for five long years.'

Jenny grasps to find the legal flaw in Eva's argument. 'But in the final year at university there are also external examiners.'

'Oh yeh, his buddy from the Aberdeen School came down to rubber stamp it.'

Jamal spots a pair of hiking boots inside the front door.

'Are those your boots, Ms Paterson?'

'No, my ex-boyfriend left them behind.'

'Do you ever wear them?'

Eva screws up her face. 'Sometimes.'

'Could you give us his name?'

'Peter Macdonald. He teaches Geography at Drumchapel High School. When he's not there he's usually playing table tennis. That's one of the reasons we split up – he's addicted. The real reason of course is that I'm a failure.'

Jamal asks, 'Would you mind if we take the hiking boots away with us? We'll bring them back as soon as possible.'

'No way.'

'Would you prefer us to return next week with a search warrant?' Jamal replies a bit too aggressively.

'Take them if you want. Take everything. I've got nothing to hide.'

*

'How did you two get on out at Carbeth? It's quite a special place, isn't it?'

'Very,' responds Jenny.

'So, can we rule out Eva Paterson?'

'I'd think so, boss. She's nice and her cat, Charbon, is so cute…'

Jamal interrupts, 'She had a pair of size eight boots which I've handed over to forensics.'

Alistair breezes in looking like the cat who got the cream, carrying a pitching wedge golf club.

'I have a seriously good lead. In fact, I'd go as far as to say I think I've found our man.'

'Tell me?'

'Jason Tully, the brother of the nurse who pronounced him dead at the scene.'

'I thought she travelled there alone.'

'That's what she said in her original statement but she was captured on cctv walking with him towards Clydeview an hour before the lecture. She lied because she "didn't want to get him into trouble".'

'And is he trouble?'

'Definitely. A background check tells us he's still on probation after serving a two year prison sentence for serious assault.'

'Oh, boy!'

'Police records show he's five foot ten and slightly built but strong.'

'Do you have an address?'

'Yes, he lives doon the watter.'

*

DI Gunn and DC Boyle enter a traditional bar on the seafront at Dunoon having been redirected there by Jason Tully's next door neighbour.

They recognise him immediately from their photograph as he is the only man in the bar with striking red hair and matching beard. Lorna walks over and, subtly showing her ID, indicates to sit down on a stool opposite.

'Mind if we sit here?'

Jason puts down his book, *From Bauhaus to Our House* by Tom Wolfe, 'Oh no, what do you lot want?'

'We're here about the murder of the architect Richard Baird.'

'All I ken is ma wee sister tried to save him.'

'And we know you were in the vicinity when he was murdered.'

'You lot are clutching at straws if I'm yer best lead.'

'Seems an odd thing for a man like you to do,' replies DI Gunn, 'taking a trip up there.'

'It was an Open Day. There's no law against going along to a building when ye've been invited.'

'What made you want to go there?'

'I saw a poster in the library. I'm interested in modern architecture - in that I hate it. The "resort" was a dump even when it was new. Leakin' straight away it was. I know because I worked on it when I was an apprentice. I'm with Charlie Boy on the subject of architecture.'

'Who?' asks Alistair.

'You mean Prince Charles?' Lorna recently visited Dumfries House, the stately home he saved in Cumnock.

Jason nods and sips his pint of heavy. 'The very one.'

'What type of work do you do Mr Tully?'

'I'm a sparky to trade but I'd prefer te work with animals.' Two white eyes belonging to a black husky dog gaze up at them from underneath the table. The dog's chin doesn't leave the floor. As DI Gunn gazes downwards she notices Jason's enormous steel toe capped boots.

He takes another sip, 'A dog handler in the police would have been my ideal job. D'ye think you could put in a good word?'

'Jason, have you put on weight recently?' asks Alistair focusing on their interviewee's rather substantial beer belly.

'Maybe a couple of stone. You're a bit cheeky are ye no?'

'Shoe size?'

Jason winks at Lorna, 'Are you fae a dating agency? Eleven and a half. Why?'

Lorna, realising his weight alone must rule him out asks, 'Did you see anything at all that day at Clydeview that might be significant?'

'I dinnae ken if it's significant but I remember passing a right bonny lass pushing an auld bike up the hill. Seemed as fit as a fiddle. She was wearing a pair o' dungarees which I thought was odd for her age.'

'And roughly what age was she?' asks Alistair.

'Around thirty, thirty-five. Maybe forty at a push.'

'Did you speak to her?'

'I said hello but she looked right through me. It was as if she wiz dreamin'.'

*

A listair looks up, 'Do you want the good news or the bad news, boss?'

'The good news.'

'We found an eyewitness who swears she saw Ciaran Wilson sitting in the cathedral, just before mass – mass starts at one o'clock.'

'Oh, that is very good news. It means he couldn't have done it.'

'The woman remembers him distinctly because he interrupted her prayer he was crying so loudly.

She recalls offering him a hanky "which he didn't return".'

DI Gunn notices Jenny is trying to fight back tears. 'What's the bad news?'

'Forensics have matched Eva Paterson's boots to the footprint found at the crime scene.'

'Really? That's incredible.' Lorna's facial expression shows disbelief. 'Could the ex-boyfriend have worn the boots? He likely still has a key.'

Jamal answers, 'No, his alibi is sound. He was at a table tennis tournament in Stirling, playing non-stop.'

Alistair adds, 'Not only that but the soil and plant samples found on the boots match samples taken from where the concrete fell.'

'Someone else could still have worn the boots,' points out Lorna.

'Also, the tread marks on Eva's mountain bike match ones found on the mud path leading up to the resort.'

DI Gunn's face strains, 'Oh no. The foolish girl.'

Alistair completes the final piece of the puzzle. 'Even the ex-con has turned out to be a valuable witness. Jenny and Jamal say the day they visited Eva out in Carbeth she was wearing denim dungarees. I mean how many women wear dungarees out cycling? It must have been her.'

Lorna's face strains, 'This is awful. And the Chief Inspector's due back on Monday. He'll insist we go straight out to Carbeth to arrest her.'

At lunchtime no one rushes to the canteen, not even for stovies. For once DI Gunn doesn't feel like eating. Out of all the suspects, Eva, the failed architect, and Cairan, the young, bankrupt architect, were the ones no one wanted to be implicated. Jamal blames himself; if he hadn't used his computer programming skills no one would even have suspected Eva. This is Jamal's first murder case and the culprit hasn't turned out to be the type of person he was expecting. He rather liked Eva Paterson and had wanted to stay longer in her homely hut.

They are all dejected leaving the police station. Jamal and Jenny, never having socialised together before, go to the nearest pub to drown their sorrows. DI Gunn pops into the city centre to do a bit of late night shopping to take her mind off the inevitable. She buys a few clothing items she hopes her daughter will like and a book for Colin. And, with all this drama Alistair doesn't know how he is going to focus on his golf match. Winning the club championship no longer seems so important.

PART THREE
CONCRETE CONCLUSION

'That's you won, Alistair. There's nothing else I can do but pick up.' Alistair returns the flag to its hole and walks towards his opponent holding out his arm. The two men shake hands at the edge of the 16th green.

'Thanks for the game, Eddie. It was a good match.'

'You played well. You drove particularly well today except when you sliced it into the field at the 12th.'

'Thanks for reminding me.'

'Do you want to play in the remaining holes?'

'Yeh, sure.'

Reaching the 18th green, the golfers shake hands again; they go into the locker room to change their shoes and pack up their clubs before chatting some more over a drink in the bar.

'I hear you're in the crime squad?'

'Yeh, but it's not as exciting as it sounds although I'm working on a interesting case at the moment.'

'I was surveying a building down at the university the other day and I saw you going into the architecture department. Are you trying to find out who killed the professor?'

'Yeh, but I can't talk about it.'

'Everyone I spoke to is glad to see the back of him. What an ego.'

'I know, Eddie. Thankfully, my lecturers at Paisley Uni weren't like that. They were totally down to earth.'

Eddie takes a large sip of lager. 'My ancient aunt tells me his wife is one to watch.'

'In what way exactly?'

'Oh, maybe I'd better not say.' Eddie is obviously eager to impart some gossip.

'You've started so you'd better finish, Eddie. What did she tell you?'

'Well, my ancient aunt was a very fine nurse, in the days when nursing was a true vocation. She was in the Victoria Hospital recently and appalled, as she put it, "at the way she was manhandled".'

'Eddie, I'll need to get going soon. What did she say about Professor Baird's wife?'

'Well, it's not about his wife exactly. It was about her famous uncle, Dr Euan Campbell.' He takes another sip of his pint and licks his lips. 'Or, as the people in the know called him – Dr Frankenstein.'

'What?'

'Her uncle was the main man at a mental hospital in Cleveland, Ohio in America and was supposed to be one of the most brilliant psychiatrists of his generation. In the world.'

'Are you making this up, Eddie?'

'Nope. Wish I was.' He takes a few big gulps of his pint in case his wife shows up to collect him early. 'My aunt was one of the dedicated nurses he chose from Glasgow Royal Infirmary to assist him in his work.'

'What, she worked for him in America?'

'Yes, but she returned home after two months.'

'What happened?'

'She saw the horrific experiments he was doing on his patients. It was supposedly for their own good but my aunt thought otherwise. They were like Euan Campbell's guinea pigs, being experimented on without their consent, unaware of the huge risks – to their sanity.'

'What was he doing to them?'

'Really sick stuff. He tried to erase his patients' memories by giving them strong electric shocks. Some of the patients couldn't remember anything afterwards and were returned to the state of a baby. Another thing he was into in a big way was hypnosis. He used to deprive them of sleep and play a tape over and over to hypnotise them.'

'Hypnosis?' A shiver runs down Alistair's spine. 'Listen, Eddie. I've got to go. I promised Susie I'd put the kids to bed. Thanks for the game.' Alistair grabs his car keys and heads straight for his car.

*

Stalling for time before the inevitable arrest of Eva Paterson, and not considering her to be a danger to anyone else, DI Gunn sets about accessing Eva's medical records.

'I can't possibly show you Eva Paterson's medical records. They're confidential.'

'Look, Dr Small,' DI Gunn has finally managed to get through to the GP's surgery, 'either you hand them over now or we apply for a court order.'

'You've got a nerve threatening me like this.'

'This is a murder enquiry, Dr Small. We have reason to suspect Eva is somehow involved.'

'What?'

'Can I come over now to take a look at Eva's file?'

'If you must.' She slams down the phone.

Reluctantly, Dr Small offers DI Gunn a quiet room to study Eva Paterson's file. She scan reads the opinions of several psychiatrists and psychologists. None of them is favourable and anti-depressants always recommended. It becomes clear Eva has suffered from depression since the age of twenty-four in varying degrees. Her first visit to the doctor, citing anxiety, came one month after failing the course the first time. Eva has been taking anti-depressants in various doses ever since. Recently she had been referred to a hypnotherapist.

Lorna returns to the doctor's consulting room to hand back the file.

'Dr Small, I see you've recommended Eva attend a hypnotherapist. Do you know if she went?'

'I recommended it, yes. We'd tried everything else. Unfortunately, these things are only available privately but I do recall her saying her boyfriend might be willing to pay for it.'

'Did you recommend any particular therapist to her?'

'Yes I did. I always recommend the same person. She's the best in Glasgow.'

'And who might she be?'

'Dr Dr Lamont. She has a practice in...'

DI Gunn is able to finish his sentence, '... Bearsden?'

*

'Does the name Eva Paterson mean anything to you?' DI Gunn is standing once again in Trudy Lamont's office.

'She's a client of mine. One who suffers badly from anxiety.'

'You must have known she hated your husband.'

Shaking her head rapidly, Trudy replies, 'The architecture course had nothing to do with it.'

'Well, what do you think caused her anxiety?'

'Eva had an extremely difficult childhood, Inspector. Her father was a controlling, chauvinistic bully. He's dead now thank goodness but even that doesn't stop Eva's painful memories...'

'Funny she never mentioned this to her GP.'

'Her father threatened her with physical punishment if she talked about the family outside the home.'

DI Gunn tries to give the impression she believes her. 'Oh, I see.'

'That's the real reason Eva is so anxious. It's not all to do with failing to become an architect. There are many contributing factors and, I am confident, I have helped her to conquer her demons.'

'That's good to know, but did you not think to divulge to Eva who you were married to?'

'I did not think it relevant, Inspector. I am a professional in my own right.'

DI Gunn phones DI Boyle as soon as she is back out on to the street.

'How d'you get on last night, Alistair?'

'I won.'

'Oh, well done. You've made it to the final then?'

'Yeh, I've got to play a guy with a handicap of plus two.'

'You've lost me. Listen, Alistair. I've discovered something very interesting. Turns out Eva Paterson is one of Trudy Lamont's clients. What do you think of that?'

'Incredible, but wait till you hear what I've found out.'

'What?'

'The guy I played golf with told me Trudy Lamont's uncle was a famous psychiatrist. Guess what he was a world expert in?'

'Sleep disorders?'

'Close. He was a world expert in experimental hypnosis, except his patients didn't know they were being experimented on.'

'Oh, Alistair. That's unbelievable.'

'Isn't it?'

'Have you put Jamal onto this yet?'

'He's already found out all he can online. Former patients, decades later, received compensation but we can't find the original newspaper articles because it was too long ago.'

'Alistair, we need to return to old-fashioned methods. Meet me at the Mitchell Library at Charing Cross in one hour.'

*

The two detectives sit awaiting their turn at the information desk on the ground floor of the Mitchell Library.

'This brings back happy memories.' DI Gunn looks up at the beautifully painted dome ceiling.

'It's a stunning building, isn't it?'

'Yeh, awesome, boss, especially when it's lit up at night.'

'When my friends and I used to come here to study we actually wrote our essays by hand.'

Alistair laughs. 'No way.'

Finally, it is their turn to be served.

'We're looking for newspaper articles on a doctor from Glasgow who became the head of a state psychiatric hospital in Cleveland, Ohio around thirty to forty years ago.'

The young, fresh-faced library assistant explains, 'If you type a search term into the text box there and hit the enter button, any related articles will be returned.'

'Do we not need a library card or password?' Alistair asks.

'No, this is a reference library. Anyone can come in here and look up information,' she explains before moving on to the next waiting customer.

'Come on, Sherlock. Hurry up.'

Alistair takes a deep breath and types in, 'Dr Euan Campbell Glasgow' and hits the search button. They wait. Slowly, article upon article is listed referencing his name.

'I trust you to organise the printouts, Alistair.'

'Why, where are you going?'

'The library café. I've heard it's pretty good.'

Alistair makes his way to the café with a huge pile of papers under his arm. While photocopying the newspaper articles he has already clocked their salacious content.

'I've bought you a sandwich and a scone.'

'I'm more interested in reading these articles.'

'That's why you're so slim, Alistair.'

He hands her a pile of papers. 'Here. You take this half. Let's find a study area and work our way through them.'

As she presses the button to summon the elevator Lorna reminisces about the times she frequented the library in the distant past, with young men even younger than Alistair. An image of her younger self flashes before her as the two glide upwards with an optimistic feeling they might be onto something.

'You take a seat there, Alistair. I'll be better here nearer the window as I've forgotten to bring my reading glasses.'

'Ok, will do.'

The pair begin wading through the newspaper articles but it doesn't take long to gather a picture of Trudy Lamont's uncle, a brilliant Scottish doctor, once revered, even idolised, but now discredited. The most recent articles focus on out-of-court settlements paid out by the American government to former patients.

'Boss, it says the psychiatric hospital was secretly financed by the CIA.'

'No way.'

Alistair continues reading, 'Patients, some with only mild forms of depression, were sent to the hospital where Euan Campbell performed experiments on them.'

'What type of experiments?' DI Gunn asks, not wanting to hear the answer.

'Intense electroshock therapy up to thirty times the normal power and he also experimented with various paralytic drugs including LSD. His work was part of the now infamous MKUltra mind control program.'

'What? And Trudy Lamont's uncle was running this horror show?'

Alistair looks up, 'Eddie's aunt said he was rotten to the core.'

'Please, keep reading.'

'Former patients suffered incontinence, amnesia and in the worst cases were reduced to the state of a baby. That's what Eddie told me.'

DI Gunn shakes her head. 'And some people only went in with mild depression.'

Alistair continues, 'His "psychic driving" experiments involved putting his patients into a drug-induced coma while playing tape loops repeating simple statements.'

'Sounds like hypnosis.'

'It is the opinion of a guy high up in the US army, now ninety, that the "psychic driving" experiments were about trying to programme people to perform actions at another's command. The method, if successful, was intended to be used by military personnel. The hope was the subjects would have no recollection afterwards of having done anything.'

Alistair leans back in the seat. 'It looks like anyone who speaks out against the MKUltra program dies shortly afterwards. The former army commander was dead within a month.'

DI Gunn concludes, 'It's possible the prof's wife knew how to programme Eva to do something she was unaware of. Trudy Lamont could have suggested, under hypnosis, that Eva go to the derelict cinema building. She could have instructed Eva to climb to the floor above at the time her husband was due to give his speech and to press down the lever to set the concrete rolling over the edge. She'd been at the architecture school six years. Eva would have recognised Richard Baird's voice.'

'It seems far-fetched and I don't know how we could prove it in court, but didn't the ex-con say Eva "had a dreamy look on her face".' Alistair flips open his notebook. 'He said, and I quote, "it was as if she wiz dreamin'".'

An announcement is made over the tannoy. The library will be closing in five minutes. The timing is perfect. They have what they came for.

'Come on, Alistair. We need to find out if the professor's wife and her famous uncle ever came into contact with one another but first we need to establish if Trudy Lamont is telling the truth about Eva's father.'

*

'When Jamal typed Ronald Paterson into Google the only things that came up were his name listed amongst Mount Florida Bowling Club competition results and a page of soppy condolence messages attached to his obituary in the local rag.'

Alistair sits facing his senior. He flicks over a page in his notebook.

'From the Census records we found out he worked as a fitter.'

'So was my father - in the shipyards.'

'This guy worked as a pump fitter at Weir's in Cathcart for thirty-nine years without a single day's absence.'

'Tragic.'

'What's more tragic is he died a year later.'

'Any trace of him in our police records?'

'No. None at all.'

DI Gunn straightens a pile of papers on her desk. 'Let's take a drive out to Mount Florida. Try and find someone who knew him.'

'We don't want to be going there at this time, boss.'

'Why not?'

'Well, Scotland are playing tonight at Hampden. It's a big game against Poland. The traffic'll be a nightmare. It doesn't make sense to take the Passat.'

'What about catching a train from Pollokshields East?'

'Nah. All the trains'll be hoaching.'

'Well, unless we manage to figure out within the next few days how Cruella Deville is involved in this sorry tale, we're going to have to arrest Eva Paterson. We need to get to Mount Florida somehow, Alistair. And pretty damn quick.'

Alistair, fast off his sporty toes, sprints out of the police station and runs along the road to the busy junction. When he spots a taxi available for hire he leaves the safety of the pavement and edges out into the road waving his arms around to catch the attention of the driver. The cab pulls over.

The chatty taxi driver and Alistair are practically on first name terms by the time DI Gunn collapses onto the seat beside him. As soon as the back door slams shut, the cab speeds off in search of Mount Florida Bowling Club.

They arrive in Carmunnock Road amidst a sea of men, women, boys and girls wearing Scotland scarfs and jerseys. Some jokers are wearing See You Jimmy hats (a tartan tammy with ginger hair hanging out from beneath it) with blue and white Saltire flags painted on their faces and large, yellow flags wrapped around their shoulders showing the Lion Rampant. Many have donned kilts for the occasion and the streets are awash with vibrant colour – mainly blue and yellow. They are all marching towards Hampden. Alistair looks at his watch. Only ten minutes to kick off. How he wishes he was going. No one is entering the bowling club which is a low, white building set back from the main road.

DI Gunn and DC Boyle go through a green wrought iron gate into a haven of calm. They walk past two immaculate grass bowling greens, climb a few stairs and enter a deserted clubhouse. Inside is a lone figure at the bar – the barman. He grudgingly puts down his book.

'Hello, I'm DI Gunn.' Lorna flashes her ID. 'And this is Detective Constable Boyle.'

'Oh, right. How can I help you?'

Alistair holds out a photograph. 'Can you tell me if you know this man?'

'Eh, Ron Paterson. He's deid. Died last year. Did youz not know that?'

'Yes, we know that,' answers Alistair. 'This is in connection with his daughter.'

'Is Eva in some kind of trouble?'

'I can't say, Mr..?'

'Rennie. She's a bonnie lass is Eva. A right nice girl. So wiz her faither. It broke his heart to see the way she ended up.'

'How did she "end up"?' asks DI Gunn.

'Unemployed and living in a hut after all they years studying at the university and all the debt she got into... Well, it wasnae worth it, was it?'

'Would you say Eva was a disappointment to her father, Mr Rennie?'

'Please, call me Doug.'

'Well, was she a disappointment?'

'Oh, aye. Cause she could have done any'hin'. She was a right clever girl, tae. She might even a' been the heid girl at Shawlands Academy. But you'd hae te check up on that.'

'Yes, you're right she was. Do you think her father might have been angry when she failed to become an architect? Did he push her too hard do you think?'

'Doubt it. Ron telt me it was the heid honcho at the university he was mad at. Ron said there wiz nothing wrong with her work. But a faither would say that.'

'So you don't think he blamed her?'

'Naw.'

'Did you consider Ron Paterson to be a violent man?'

'Whit? Nooo. He wouldnae harm a fly. If anything he wiz henpecked. His wife came to some of the functions here.'

'Do you know if he had a difficult relationship with his daughter?'

'Doubt it. I thought they were real close but no in an unhealthy way or any'hin'. Naw he was a braw man. I doubt if you'd find anybody around here speak badly of him, but don't take my word for it.'

'Okay, Doug. You've been very helpful.' Lorna glances up at an enormous television in the corner. 'Any reason you aren't showing the game tonight?'

'The club stopped paying for the SKY Sports channels. I told them at the time it was a big mistake.'

As they leave the building a loud cheer breaks the silence of the night.

'Brilliant. Scotland must have scored,' exclaims Alistair.

'Wonders never cease.'

They make their way to the nearest taxi rank which has plenty of taxis but none with a driver. A punter, standing at the entrance of the pub opposite, calls to someone inside. A middle-aged man drags himself away from a television screen and returns to his car. Lorna and Alistair jump in the back and just as the driver pulls away, another, not so loud cheer is heard.

The driver says, 'Oh, naw. That's them equalised already.'

*

'Why is it, Alistair, architects nearly always live in old houses?'

'Because they've got a bit of character and are better built?'

'This one is a beauty.' DI Gunn presses the antique doorbell of an impressive town house in one of the best streets in Dowanhill.

'And look at this stunning stained glass. It looks original too.'

'*Islands in the Stream* Dolly Parton.' Alistair opens the letter box. The music becomes louder. They hear a man and woman laughing. 'Sounds like she has company.' He presses the button more aggressively. Finally lady-like footsteps make their way towards them.

The large oak-paneled, stained-glass door moves inwards. Trudy Lamont stands clutching a champagne glass. The animated expression disappears from her beautifully made up face.

'Inspector Gunn. What are you doing here?'

'We have a warrant to search your house.'

'What??? Why???? You won't find anything here.'

A man, with a snooty Glasgow accent calls out, 'Trudy?' Stuart Milne, the front runner in the race to become the next head of school, stumbles into the hall singing, "*Making love to each other, ah ha!*" He stops abruptly and stares at the two police officers as the record continues to play in the background.

Trudy regains her composure. 'You'd better come in. But, please don't damage any artwork or antiques.'

Having finally managed to park the car, two uniformed officers appear and run up the front steps and gain entry along with their colleagues.

'Try the attic first, boys.'

Several old-fashioned suitcases line the attic walls. They are the type of suitcases which could be up-cycled if one could be bothered. Sergeant Hammond flips two metal fastenings upwards to open the first suitcase and quickly ascertains it holds only old sheets and blankets. A second suitcase holds a collection of 78 rpm vinyl records. A third houses a collection of dolls.

Moving on round the attic, he opens a large hat box full of birthday cards and letters. A pile, beautifully wrapped in brown paper and ribbon, takes pride of place amongst less organised bundles.

DI Gunn pokes her head through the attic hatch pointing her torch at Sergeant Hammond.

'Any luck yet, Martin?'

'Maybe. I might have found something here.'

'What is it?'

'The name you're looking for is here. There's a bundle of airmail letters from a Euan Campbell addressed to a Mrs Alice Lamont, all with a USA postage stamp. The address at the top of each letter is Ohio State Psychiatric Hospital, Cleveland, Ohio, USA.'

'Well done, Martin.'

'Who is Alice Lamont, boss?'

'Alice Lamont was Dr Euan Campbell's sister. She was the only sibling he stayed in touch with. Alice was the mother of our party girl downstairs. Better put them in a plastic bag and take them down the station to examine them thoroughly.'

*

DI Gunn unties the knot of ribbon and settles down to reading the pile of letters.

'There's a flat white for you, boss. Am I right you've switched from lattes?'

'Yes, it has fewer calories. Thanks, Alistair.'

'How many letters are there?'

'Too many. They wrote to each other over a twenty year period. Trudy was eighteen and had just started training to be a doctor at Glasgow Uni when he died peacefully in his sleep.'

'Typical.'

'He starts each letter with a paragraph describing the weather.'

'Is it better than Scotland's?'

'Then a little about what his wife has been doing, like making apple pie or homemade soup, although her soup is "never as good as their own mother's" who apparently added a pile of salt. He goes into the academic achievements of each of his six children.'

'Maybe I should have got you a double expresso.'

'Oh, here's something interesting. He's invited Trudy to visit the family in Cleveland and offered to pay her plane fare.'

'So, she went to America.'

'That's you presuming, Alistair. Look, I was invited by a handsome Turk I met in the upstairs bar of the Ubiquitous Chip to go to Turkey. I didn't go.'

Returning her thoughts to the task at hand, Lorna continues to scan read the letters. Subsequent ones confirm that, despite never having set foot outside Scotland, Trudy does take up his offer.

'Alistair, I've found it. I've found the link.'

'What happened in America?'

'It turns out that she didn't get on with her cousins. They were too childish for her. Being an only child she was more used to adult company. And guess which adult she bonded with?'

'Frankenstein?'

'Bingo. He writes here, *It is wonderful getting to know my niece. Alice, you have done a fine job since you dispensed with her layabout father.*'

'And listen to this, *She is such a clever girl and what has astounded me is that she is taking such a keen interest in my work. If only my wife would show the same level of interest.*'

'And this is the best bit, *She has been shadowing me at the institute, learning about my methods to deepen the power of hypnosis in order to cure the mentally ill, or during war-time, to programme soldiers to carry out tasks they are unaware of. Of course, the last part you must keep to yourself, dear Alice. As Churchill says, "Careless talk costs lives".*'

'And not only that. She wrote the instructions down. *My delightful niece is a born student, Alice. She has taken copious notes of everything I have shown her in my laboratory and I can tell she has every ability to make it to university to study medicine. She needs to stick in at school and stay clear of that scallywag Richard Baird who seems to be pestering her at school. Trudy tells me he won't take no for an answer.*'

'Do you think we have enough evidence to prove she was somehow involved?'

'Not yet. Ask Jenny and Jamal to check out her phone records, bank statements etc. We still need somehow to place her at the scene of the crime. Also find out whether Eva went that morning to

Trudy Lamont's office, and you go and talk to the ex-boyfriend.'

*

Table tennis players of all ages, colour and sizes, male and female with faces showing deep concentration smash tiny white balls at each other. Between points referees call out running scores. Around the walls of Drumchapel sports hall more people sit crushed up on gym benches eagerly awaiting their turn.

A fit-looking blonde-haired man in his early thirties, wearing a club tracksuit, walks across the hall towards DC Boyle, the obvious stranger in town, standing awkwardly by the door. Alistair wishes he had come to play table tennis.

'Are you interested in joining?'

'No. Well, yes, but it's not what I'm here for. I'm looking for Peter Macdonald.'

'That's me.'

'Oh, ok. I need to talk to you about Eva Paterson.'

Peter stops smiling.

'Are you from the Department of Social Security? I know for a fact she's towing the line now.'

'No, I'm not. This is potentially more serious.' Alistair subtly shows his ID. 'I'm Detective Constable Boyle.'

Peter's face shows panic. 'Is she all right?'

'Let's go outside.'

They leave the building as another crowd of youngsters enter.

'What's this about?'

'We're trying to eliminate Eva from a murder enquiry,' replies Alistair.

'What? You're joking. Whose murder?'

'I'm afraid I'm not joking. I'm investigating the murder of Professor Richard Baird, the architect.'

'Oh, that's ridiculous. She hated the guy, yes, but I've never known Eva to be physically aggressive.' Peter shakes his head.

'Is it true you paid for Eva to have hypnotherapy sessions?'

'Yes. So? I was trying to help her.'

'What do you think is wrong with her?'

'Eva has never got over being failed at the end of the architecture course. She's been more or less unemployed ever since. Now they're making her work for a pissy amount of dole money. That'd make anyone ill.'

'The private hypnotherapy sessions must have been expensive for you?'

'To begin with yes, when Eva went to the woman's office in Bearsden but then she offered her telephone sessions at a reduced rate. Said they were just as effective. I suppose it makes sense as it's her voice Eva was listening to; she didn't need to see her.'

'Do you know when these telephone sessions took place?'

'Since she's been stacking shelves in the pound shop I think they've been on Saturday mornings. I couldn't say for sure. We've kind of split up, but, between you and me, I am secretly hoping to get back together. You've got to believe me, you couldn't meet a nicer person. She's just a bit depressed.'

'Peter, it's not me you have to convince.'

*

DI Gunn stands by her faithful whiteboard, marker in one hand and a cup of coffee in the other. Eva's face has been replaced by Trudy Lamont's.

'So what have you all got for me today?'

Jamal replies, 'Trudy Lamont made a phone call to Eva at eleven a.m. on the day her husband was killed.'

Alistair adds, 'And she wasn't just phoning Eva to make an appointment like Trudy has claimed. She called Eva to perform a hypnotherapy session on her. The call lasted a full forty-five minutes. We can all guess what that programming session involved and Eva could have cycled from Carbeth and reached Dumbarton before one p.m.'

'Jenny, you've been out again to interview Eva, haven't you?'

'Yes, and she has no recollection of having been to the Clydeview Resort that day although she did visit it as a student. That's where Professor Baird overheard her saying, "I've been inside more attractive multi-storey car parks," the comment she reckons cost her her career. Eva was so shocked when I told her what we had found out that she was physically sick. I don't think she's lying, boss. The only thing she remembers from that day is hearing Trudy's voice telling her to deeply relax.'

DI Gunn points at Trudy Lamont's face. 'She is behind it, I know she is, but we still can't prove she was at the crime scene prior to that fateful day. But she must have been. Someone must have placed the concrete lintel at the hole's edge above.'

DI Gunn points at the little bag holding a tiny fleck of blue plastic. 'And what about this? What does that remind you of?'

Jenny answers, 'Going swimming. The overshoes for walking round a pool.'

'Right, well find out if Trudy Lamont goes swimming and, if so, where?'

Jamal says, 'She made a phone call exactly one week earlier to the AA breakdown service. The call was made halfway between Dumbarton and Glasgow.'

DI Gunn taps the side of her nose. 'The location is interesting. Jamal, contact the AA. Find out who went out that day to help her.'

Jamal catches up with AA man Jack Davis on a quiet side street in Pollokshields. As Jamal parks his car he sees a young couple step into a classic mini and wave happily as they drive off. Jack smiles and returns the wave. He places papers in a compartment situated at the back of his bright yellow motorbike.

Jamal locks his car and crosses the wide, peaceful street. He smiles as he approaches the man who, on closer inspection, must be pushing sixty.

'Hello there, mate. Your controller told me I'd catch you here.'

'Did she?'

Jamal produces his ID, 'I need to ask you a few questions.'

His face drops, 'What's this about?'

'It's about this woman.' Jamal produces a photograph of Trudy Lamont.'

'Oh, yes. I remember the dame. Quite attractive. Drove a Mazda MX5 convertible. What's she supposed to have done?'

'I can't say but I'm from the Serious Crime Squad.'

'Good grief.'

'Could you tell me why she called the AA?'

'Her car broke down.'

'I know that, but what was wrong with it?'

'A flat tyre. And like most of the new cars nowadays it didn't have a spare tyre so I had to use the temporary repair kit. Piece of nonsense. Dangerous if you ask me.'

'How would you describe her demeanour?'

'Friendly. Chatty.'

'Did she seem excitable at all?'

'No, she seemed calm enough.'

'Do you remember the type of clothes she was wearing?'

'Dressy. Wore a lot of make-up. What I did notice though, was that one of her diamond earrings was missing. I mentioned it to her and we had a scout around looking for it but couldn't find it.'

'Was she upset?'

'Not overly. She was surprisingly cool about it. Said she'd put in an insurance claim.'

'Thank you,' replies Jamal, 'I won't take up any more of your time.'

'Good, because I've got to scoot. A woman in Pollok has managed to lock her key in the car boot and a Pug with breathing problems is trapped inside.' Jack puts his leg over the motorbike, secures his helmet and zooms off.

*

Jenny is about to enter the Victorian swimming pool at 61 Arlington Street when she notices the young wine waiter from The Blythswood. He is walking, or more like skipping, towards her carrying a portfolio case. She watches as he optimistically reaches up to touch the branch of a tree. He is grinning like a child and when he finally notices Jenny his blue eyes light up.

'Hi, Aaron.' Jenny has always been good at remembering names.

'Hi there.'

'Have you had some good news?' she asks knowing full well he must have.

'Why d'you say that?'

'Have you got a job in an architect's office or something?'

'How do you know?'

'I've been listening in to all your phone calls.'

Aaron's smile drops.

'Duh. I could tell by looking at your face and you're carrying a portfolio case.'

He cheers up. 'Oh, of course.'

'That's brilliant.' Jenny is truly happy for him.

'It was a night I volunteered to help out at the Mackintosh lecture in Ruchill Church Hall that did it.'

'Really?'

'Yeh, an architect said if a vacancy came up in his firm he'd give me a call. I thought he was bullshitting me.'

'Just shows you,' replies Jenny.

'Listen, do you fancy going for a drink with me to celebrate? Or are you working?'

Jenny's head moves backwards, her face displaying surprise. 'What?'

'Or do you have a boyfriend?'

'No, it's not that. No I don't. But yes, I am working and tonight I've got to go somewhere with my workmates.'

'Oh, ok.' Aaron Guthrie can take a hint.

'But… if you give me your number Aaron, I'll text you and we could meet up some other time.'

'Sounds good.' He speedily pulls out his mobile phone. They swap numbers and say their goodbyes. As he continues to skip along the road Jenny manages to regain her composure before entering the Arlington Baths to ask some serious questions.

The reception area is empty but a young woman, wearing a pinafore, is polishing the racing green tiles. She stops, holds the cloth in mid-air and turns to face Jenny.

'Can I help you?' Her accent is foreign.

Jenny produces her ID. 'Would it be possible to speak to the manager?'

'I don know. I see if he around.'

The cleaner leaves to try to find him, giving Jenny an opportunity to look around. She smiles when she notices swimming trunks hanging up on pegs on the wall. She opens a double-door and sees dozens of pairs of shoes lined up neatly in rows. Beyond the "shoe corridor" is an appealing view of an old-fashioned swimming pool. She hears the sound of someone diving in.

A tall, well-built, unsmiling man appears, suggesting the cleaner's English is good enough to pass on the fact the police are here asking questions.

'Hello. How can I help?'

Jenny shows her ID and pulls out a photograph of Trudy Lamont from her pocket.

The manager's face hardens. 'This is a private member's club and we value our member's privacy.'

'This is a murder enquiry, Mr?'

'Milne.' Jenny writes this down in her little black notebook.

'First name?'

'Thomas.'

Holding out the photo again, Jenny asks, 'Mr Milne, do you recognise this woman?'

'Yes, it's Trudy Lamont... Richard's wife. I saw on the news...'

'Did you know them?'

'Yes, they are... were both members here but it was him I saw more often. He swam every morning before work.'

'Do you keep a register of when people come and go?'

'Yes, it's right here.' He gestures to a large leather diary lying open showing today's date and a list of names with times in and out.

'Could you tell me when Trudy Lamont last visited?'

'She's not been back since she lost her husband.' He flicks the pages of the diary backwards. 'Here she is on Tuesday 29th March.' He continues flicking backwards. 'And again on the 22nd at a similar time.' Looks like she came once a week, on Tuesdays… Here she is again on Tuesday 15th.'

'Mr Milne, do you provide blue, disposable plastic overshoes?'

Thomas Milne screws up his large, hard-working face. 'Yes, I ask people to put them on over their shoes when I'm giving them a tour of the club, but they're not disposable, we do recycle them.'

'Would you mind if I took away one of those shoe coverings?'

'Sure.' Thomas seizes the opportunity to entice a new member. 'Have you been here before?'

'Never. I used to live around the corner on Woodlands Road when I was at uni and I didn't even know it was here.'

'Why don't I give you a quick tour now? You can take a plastic overshoe away with you afterwards?'

'I'd love to have a look around,' responds Jenny enthusiastically.

Thomas Milne holds open the door leading to the inner sanctum.

'With your type of work you would benefit from relaxing in our facilities here. Quite a few of Glasgow's Finest are members.' Then, on seeing Jenny's unfavourable reaction, adds, 'And lots of members are from the islands. Let me guess. Are you from Lewis?'

'Yeh, from Stornoway, but I've lived in Glasgow for ten years.'

'But a beautiful accent never fades.'

At the end of the members' shoe corridor Thomas Milne pulls two plastic shoe covers from a dispenser and hands them to Jenny.

They enter the pristine, chlorine-smelling pool area where a young man swings over the pool from trapeze hoops dangling from the ceiling. A few good swimmers pound up and down the marked lanes. The crystal clear, sky blue pool is brightly lit overhead by a pitched, glazed roof supported by timber trusses. Jenny is impressed.

By the time they reach the entrance to the Turkish suite, the room most steeped in history, Jenny is considering joining. Through the glass door she glimpses a stunning tiled room with an Arabian blue painted beehive roof punctured by red and blue star-shaped windows producing stunning coloured shafts of light. Several women, their heads and bodies wrapped in thick, white towels relax with their eyes closed on wooden slatted reclining chairs.

Jenny is about to open her mouth to reveal her interest when Thomas Milne utters a deal-breaking club rule.

'There's no talking allowed in this space.'

As he opens the door he whispers, 'Silence must be maintained in here at all times.'

Jenny glances at her watch. Now, feeling a pang of guilt, she makes her excuses to make a quick getaway. Besides, she has to prepare for heading out tonight to the spooky Clydeview Resort to hunt for a tiny diamond.

*

'Trudy Lamont could have lost her earring anywhere, boss.'

'Yes, I know Alistair, but she could have lost it here,' points out DI Gunn.

'Shine the torch over here please, Jamal.'

It's nightfall, the sound of owls permeate the creepy, derelict resort. DI Gunn, Alistair, Jenny and Jamal, wearing coverings over their shoes and hands, search around the undergrowth close to the area from where the concrete lintel had fallen.

'It worked for my dad,' Jamal says, hopefully. Jamal's father once camped out all night on Ben Lomond to find his wife's lost diamond engagement ring which he found under a patch of wild thistles.

DI Gunn, losing heart, says, 'It was a good idea Jamal, but I don't think we're going to be so lucky this time.'

'Don't you think it's significant that Trudy Lamont hasn't yet put in an insurance claim?' says Jenny.

'Boss! Boss! what's that glistening over there?'

DI Gunn pins a photograph of the diamond earring up on the white board.

'Thanks to this little beauty we can now place Trudy Lamont at the scene of the crime.'

'Not only that, boss.' Jenny is beaming. 'Forensics found the bit of blue plastic matches the overshoes they use at Arlington Baths where she happens to be a member. The initials AB are printed onto each polythene sole and under a microscope it is possible to see, faintly, the apex of the letter A imprinted on a piece of dried mud found at the crime scene.'

'That would also explain why she left no footprints.' DI Gunn doesn't yet know if all this evidence will be enough to convince a jury of Trudy Lamont's guilt and Eva's innocence, but she is fairly confident Eva should receive no worse than the "not proven" verdict when the case eventually goes to trial. The verdict, unique to Scot's Law, is given when there is insufficient evidence to establish guilt or innocence.

A tanned Detective Chief Inspector Darren Russell enters carrying five cups of freshly squeezed orange juice.

'I hope all this noise means you're ready to arrest someone.'

They reply in unison, 'Yes!'

Two police cars screech into the sleepy street in Dowanhill causing blinds in adjacent town houses to twitch. The cars double park outside Trudy Lamont's home. DI Gunn and DC Boyle are first up the steps backed up by two uniformed officers. On ringing the doorbell the living room light goes out signalling someone is home. Slowly, the front door is pulled inwards revealing a very different woman to the one they had encountered previously. Gone are the high heels and make-up.

DI Gunn delivers the blow. 'Dr Dr Trudy Annabelle Lamont, I'm arresting you on suspicion of murdering your husband.' Trudy sighs a deep sigh while looking directly at Lorna. DI Gunn continues, 'There is no obligation for you to say anything until a solicitor is present.'

Trudy Lamont remains calm. 'I was expecting you, Inspector. Would you mind if I get my coat and handbag?'

'Of course not.'

Trudy's eyes focus on a pair of handcuffs being carried by a uniformed officer. 'The handcuffs won't be necessary.' She turns around and walks across the polished hallway to lift a camel jacket hanging from a carved wooden handrail at the bottom of the stairs. She places her arms inside the lined sleeves and ties the cloth belt around her waist, tugging sharply. Trudy picks up her handbag and walks back towards the open door. This isn't exactly the response the police were expecting.

'I'm ready.'

Alistair asks, 'You're ready to be arrested?'

'No,' Trudy is emphatic. 'I am ready to confess.'

*

D I Gunn and DC Boyle sit at a table in the police interview room facing Trudy Lamont and Edmund Hamilton, her lawyer. DI Gunn presses a button on a recording device.

DI Gunn: This interview is being recorded. The date is 3rd May 2016, the time is 11:20 a.m.? by my watch. I am DI Gunn and I am based at Glasgow police headquarters, Dalmarnock. I work in the Serious Crime Squad. What is your name?'

Trudy: Dr Dr Trudy Elizabeth Lamont.

DI Gunn: Is it okay to call you Trudy?

Trudy: Yes.

DI Gunn: Ok, thank you. Trudy, can you confirm your date of birth for me?

Trudy: 11 November 1957.

DI Gunn: Thank you. Also present is...

DC Boyle: DC Boyle.

DI Gunn: Also present is Trudy Lamont's lawyer...

Lawyer: Edmund Hamilton.

DI Gunn: What is your occupation, Trudy?

Trudy:	I run my own hypnotherapy practice in Bearsden called "It's all in the mind".
DI Gunn:	Is Eva Paterson one of your clients?
Trudy:	She is.
DI Gunn:	Did you call Eva Paterson at 11 a.m., two hours before the death of your husband.
Trudy:	I did.
DI Gunn:	How long did the call last?
Trudy:	Forty to forty-five minutes.
DI Gunn:	What was the purpose of the call?
Trudy:	It was a hypnotherapy session.
DI Gunn:	Did you hypnotise her?
Trudy:	She was an easy subject to hypnotise.
DI Gunn:	Please answer the question.
Trudy:	Yes.
DI Gunn:	Under hypnosis, did you suggest to Eva Paterson that she cycle to the derelict holiday resort in Dumbarton?
Trudy:	Yes I did. I told her to arrive no later than one o'clock. Eva is very punctual.
DI Gunn:	What else did you suggest?
Trudy:	I told her to climb up to the second floor and, on hearing my husband's voice, raise up the concrete lintel by stepping on the plank.
DI Gunn:	Why did you tell her to do this?
Lawyer:	Can we take a break? I'd like to speak privately with my client.
Trudy:	No, it's okay, Edmund. I want to carry on.

DI Gunn: Why did you instruct Eva to do this?

Trudy: To kill my husband.

DI Gunn: Ok. Why did you want to kill your husband?

Trudy: Because I saw first-hand, in Eva, the consequences of his barbaric approach to education.

DI Gunn: What? You didn't agree with his teaching methods?

Trudy: Methods! What methods? My husband passed the students he liked and failed the students he didn't. Everyone at his school knew that. No one under him questioned his decisions. There was no one above him.

DI Gunn: What did Eva do to anger him?

Trudy: She committed the ultimate sin, Inspector... she had the temerity to mock his masterpiece.

DI Gunn: She told you that?

Trudy: I was her therapist.

DI Gunn: Are you related to a Dr Euan Campbell whom you visited in America in your youth.

Trudy: Yes, but I had no idea then that what he was doing was wrong.

DI Gunn: You realise Eva could have gone to jail for a crime she had no recollection of.

Trudy: No. Never. I was always going to confess if Eva was charged. I made that decision at the outset.

DI Gunn: Trudy, are you having an affair with Stuart Milne?

Trudy: No, but we are close. We have a lot in common.

DI Gunn: Such as?

Trudy: We both despised the same man.

Edmund: Trudy, dear Trudy, if only he hadn't split us up in our youth.

Trudy: Oh, Edmund.

Edmund: And when I think of how much my father did for him.

Trudy: Edmund, for years now I've known that I should have spent my life with you.

DI Gunn: This interview is now terminated. The time is 11:40 a.m.

DI Gunn presses the stop button and sighs. Silence fills the room for what feels like minutes. It is Trudy who breaks it.

'I'm curious, Inspector. At what point did you suspect I might have something to do with my husband's death?'

DI Gunn rubs her chin and gazes upwards. 'It's hard to say but I suppose I suspected you before your husband was murdered.'

'Before, Inspector? What on earth do you mean?'

'Well, I had attended one of your husband's lectures.'

'Did you? That must have been dull.'

'Afterwards, when I spotted him milling about drinking wine and laughing and joking with the young women in the audience, I thought to myself, "that little nyaff has some ego".'

Trudy manages a slight smile. 'He did that.'

DI Gunn reaches her punchline. 'My next thought was if I were married to him I'd probably want to kill him.'

If you've enjoyed reading *Concrete Alibi* the author would be most grateful if you would leave a positive review on either Amazon or Goodreads. Any constructive criticism is appreciated.

Book 2 in the Inspector Gunn series is *Dental Sting*.

Cover image: Rogano restaurant, Glasgow

Detective Inspector Lorna Gunn, the arty detective, returns in *Dental Sting* to investigate another clever murder in the city of Glasgow. The dodgy professional being bumped off this time is a dentist.

Recommended if you like a good puzzle and dislike gratuitous violence.

Book 3 in the Inspector Gunn series is *Criminal Lawyer*.

Cover image: High Court of Justiciary in Glasgow

Detective Inspector Lorna Gunn investigates the sudden death of a recently retired criminal defence lawyer found slumped over a card table, having played his last ever game of Solitaire.

Includes a bit of humour, no bad language or gratuitous violence.